THE NOWHERE WITCH

DONNA AUGUSTINE

1

I'd been in my fair share of bad spots: getting stuck in the wish factory barracks, the dragon incident, the grouslie attack, getting pinned down in the Unsettled Lands with *it* trying to kill me... I could rehash the ugly situations I'd been in all day, but I wasn't looking to drag the point out. The heart of the matter was that I'd been in more unfavorable predicaments than I cared to remember. And yet any of those times were preferable to the one I was in right now. Wrists and ankles tied, having fallen on my ass with Hawk kneeling in front of me, smirking as if I'd just proven him right once and for all.

"I did warn you this would happen if you insisted on staying in Salem. How many times did I warn you?" He squinted his steel eyes as he rested a muscled forearm on a bent knee, impervious to the fifth wind that shredded the rest of us. "I know you received my messages, so why didn't you move to New York like I told you to?"

He was still handsome in that rugged, ruthless way I remembered. He had the kind of look that drew you in at your own peril. For a little while there, I'd begun to trust him more than anyone. Come to look to him for answers. I'd done the unthinkable: I'd trusted him. And he was starting off our reunion with a reminder of exactly why I'd cursed him every day of the last couple of months. He'd used me up for months, sealing the deal with a kiss, before he tossed me away because it had suited his purpose.

Like he told me to. Same Hawk, different day. He still thought I would do as he directed, like I was the lost witch who'd just landed in Xest that first time, the one he'd saved from the wish factory. All those ignored letters hadn't clued him in. Well, I wasn't the same Tippi, not by a country mile. I'd learned a lot about myself since I'd allowed him to run me out of Xest. I guess that tended to happen after enough bumps and bruises. You toughen up, you build scar tissue—you adapt and grow. I'd adapted, and I was about to give him a good lesson on exactly what I'd learned.

He stayed in his current position, saying nothing else as he waited for me to respond or say something silly, like *Oh, of course you're right. I made an error in judgment.* Hell would freeze over before that happened. Actually, considering how cold my butt was and my current situation, hell might have indeed frozen over, and it *still* wasn't going to happen. My relationship with Hawk, or the one we'd had, ended the day he'd forced me out of Xest. I would never bow to his wishes again. I'd sworn to myself if I ever managed to get back here to Xest, I would do things my way.

"I have no need for you or your lectures on where you deem I've gone wrong." I wouldn't bother filling him in on how much I'd wanted to get back here since the minute I'd left. If staying in Salem had gotten me back here, then it wasn't a mistake. I was right where I belonged, finally, after months. There was only one thing I needed from Hawk before I didn't care if I never saw him again.

I thrust out my hands. "Are you going to untie me or not?"

He pulled a knife out of his boot and then cut the rope tied around my ankles.

"If you actually knew how to listen, I'd continue to try to talk sense into you, but I know better."

As he moved to my wrists, it was obvious he was making sure none of his exposed flesh touched mine. I was all too aware of the sizzle our contact would have, and he clearly was as well. Seemed some memories lingered strong for both of us. I'd tried to bury the memory of the exhilarating sizzle a mile deep, right underneath the day he'd forced me out. So, if he was avoiding any kind of touch for my sake, he needn't bother. A little contact wasn't taking me down so easy this time around. The only contact I'd welcome would be in combat.

I got to my feet, happy I had my jacket for this abduction. Too bad I hadn't had some warning and been able to pack a bag. Not the same problem it was the first time around, when I'd been dropped with nothing but my pajamas in the middle of a place I'd never imagined. I knew what I was doing this time, and I had some means. Zab could probably transfer my money back from dollars to coins, and I'd pick up a few things tomorrow. Although I'd need a few to get a hotel tonight. Did they have hotels in Xest? Couldn't remember any, but I'd figure something out.

I also had the minor problem of someone wanting to use me again. Whoever had paid for my abduction this time hadn't been Hawk, the way Braid and Spike had taken off.

As much as limited contact with Hawk would be nice, he must've known something to show up here and now. What was he up to, anyway? He'd moved a bit away and was scraping at the ground with his boot.

"Do you know if it was Marvin again?" You'd have thought Marvin would've given up on me working in the factory, but some people would always dig in. I mean, what use would I be when all the dandelions I'd touched had blown up? If he brought me back, he might end up losing his contract for magic with... Well, whomever.

"I don't know who hired them. Someone overheard them talking about a job involving you, and they called me. I didn't get any other specifics."

It was likely Raydam. Or not. I wouldn't work with him anyway, so wouldn't he rather have me in Salem?

When I did eventually figure it out, I'd probably thank them. They'd gotten me right back where I wanted to be. When they eventually came for me again, we'd have a little chat about how things weren't going to work out the way they wanted, and it would be done.

Maybe whoever sent for me didn't really know who I was? Maybe they'd heard some rumors and thought I'd be useful and that they could use me. Although Spike and Braid had talked about how I was stronger, so the person who hired them must have known something...

Didn't matter. That was a problem for tomorrow. There was plenty enough to do tonight.

I was brushing snow off my pants, getting my bearings, when the sound of water hit my ears.

I turned around in time to see Hawk closing his flask.

Oh no, not again. That puddle better be for him alone. I was done being told where to go and what to do.

"What's that?" I asked, pointing at it like it was the doorway to hell.

"I'm taking you home," he said matter-of-factly as he tucked his flask inside his jacket.

"You're not taking me anywhere. I am home." I took a step away, emphasizing my point. The days of Hawk dictating my every move were long over. I was my own agent. Had been since the day he kicked me out of Xest.

"You're going back." He reached a hand into his pocket, looking for salt, as if his declaration was enough to make me fall in line.

I could make a run for it but didn't. Those days were over, too. If there was one thing I'd learned about myself since this all began, way back with a séance, a ghost, and a bad debt, it was that I had no taste for running. It didn't feel good, honest, or dignified. Running, to put it plainly, sucked. So did hiding, and that was all I'd done my entire life. From now on, the only time I'd be running or hiding was if a monster of biblical proportions was breathing fire at my back.

"I'm not going anywhere."

He looked at me, his expression shielded. "You are."

I was so firm on my not running that a crazy part of my brain had decided moving closer was a bright idea, because before I thought better of it, I took a few steps toward him.

His eyes ran over my face, lingering briefly on my lips, almost as if he missed me or wanted to kiss me or something. Right before they deadened again.

I wasn't sure what his game was. Maybe he thought if

he flashed a few fake emotions my way, I'd crumple. Not this time.

"I guess anywhere but Xest is where you think I should be?" I asked. He was smart enough to not answer, because I was done with his input. "You told me once I could be more. Remember that? But *more* somewhere else is what you meant. Well, here I am, and I *am* going to be more, and I'm going to do it on my terms in Xest."

If he wanted to puddle-jump me back to Salem, he'd have to drag me kicking and screaming.

"This isn't the place for you." He said it softly, as if he felt bad or something.

Another flicker of emotion, another breadcrumb to lead me away from my goal and to where he thought I should be.

I should disengage, but that was easier said than done. As much as I wanted to be unmoved in any way by Hawk, something in me always burned brighter and hotter when he was near, and it was a fire that was hard to completely snuff out.

"Give me one reason it isn't."

"I'll give you multiple. The thing in the Unsettled Lands, for one; the long list of enemies you've accumulated here. I could go on all night."

"How is that any different from your situation? We were working toward the same ends. My enemies are yours as well." It was all bull. If I had enemies, I made them by being aligned with him. Now that he was out of the equation, who knew what might happen? I might be fine with everyone.

"It just is."

That was it? *It just is*? That thing in the Unsettled Lands? I'd actually gone head to head with it and survived. But I was the one who didn't belong here because *it just is*?

Why had I ever believed anything he'd said? He wasn't worried about what was right. He only cared about what was right for him, and for whatever reason, he wanted me gone. The realization cut me like a thousand razors. I'd thought I'd hardened myself to him since I'd been gone. I had...mostly. But not quite enough. I'd get there, though. He didn't deserve my softness.

"I belong here every bit as much as you do."

I gave him my back, daring him to try to force me into that puddle as I took a good look around, trying to get my bearings. Was that the old mailbox in the distance? The one I'd used to mail my letter to Lorinda? Yes. It was. Okay, town wasn't too far from here. I could be at Zab's in under an hour. He'd help me get my money transferred back to coin and I'd go from there. I'd find a hotel next, and then a job soon after. I started walking, not looking back even as I could feel Hawk's eyes burning into me.

"Tippi, where are you going?"

"Not your problem," I said, refusing to look at him. I'd never take another order from him again.

The fifth wind blew my hair back, and I breathed in the chill like it was the first time I'd taken a real breath in months. I was finally alive again.

2

The feeling of the fifth wind had lost some of its glory by the time I reached Zab's, knocking harder than I'd meant to due to lack of feeling in my knuckles.

Zab's voice rang out from the other side. "I'm coming!"

Yeah, definitely a little too aggressive on the knock.

It swung open a couple of seconds later, and there was my dear friend standing on the threshold, spiky blue hair going in every direction as his eyes glued to mine.

He squinted for a second, as if he couldn't quite believe I was standing there. His jaw dropped but quickly morphed into a huge smile. "Tippi! Get in here!" he said, waving me into his place.

I almost hugged him but stopped short, reminding myself that people here didn't touch. I wanted nothing more than to wrap my arms around him, but that wasn't what Xesters did, and I was a Xester now. Instead I matched his smile, megawatt for megawatt.

"You look half frozen! Let me make you a tea while you tell me how you ended up back here," he said, waving me toward the couch against the wall. "I can't believe

Hawk didn't tell me you were coming. Go, sit! Get comfortable."

I didn't answer right away, stalling for time as he busied himself with tea.

His place was cute, a large studio that was slightly messy, but no worse than my own usually was. There were pictures of Xest landscapes on the walls, and it had little odd knickknacks scattered about on shelves, which made me wonder if he'd been behind at least some of the collection at the broker's office. The best thing about the place was that it was as warm and inviting as he was. It was the kind of space that made you want to curl up in the corner of his yellow couch and read a book.

He brought me the tea and settled on the opposite side of the couch.

"So what happened? Did Hawk go and get you? I knew he'd bring you back. He's been off ever since you left." Zab wasn't even sipping his tea as he waited hungrily for details.

Zab was my friend. That was a given. But he was Hawk's guy too. That was also a given. This did have the potential to get awkward, and I didn't know where Musso lived.

"Hawk didn't bring me back. Those two bumbling idiots that kidnapped me the first time grabbed me again." I sipped my tea as that little tidbit was absorbed.

"For who?" Zab asked.

"Not sure. They ran as soon as Hawk showed." Another sip, another pause as I slowly fed him the details.

"Then Hawk just showed up in the middle of the abduction?" He leaned forward. "I'm so glad you're back. Things are already more interesting."

"I'm glad I could entertain," I said, laughing. I wasn't

sure if it was actually funny or if I was exploding with nerves over whether I'd be tossed out on my ass when he found out that me and his boss weren't seeing eye to eye. A lot hinged on Zab's help. If he wasn't the man I thought he was, being back in Xest was going to be a lot tougher. Not that I'd give up.

"Are you coming back to work at the office?" Zab asked.

I wrapped my hands around the warmth of the cup, trying to thaw out while planning my next words. "No, that's unlikely."

"Why not? I thought you liked it? We always had such a good time." He leaned back a couple of inches, his chin dropping as he said, "I mean, I thought we did..."

I shook my head quickly. "We definitely did. We had a great time. I've missed you and Musso more than I thought possible. I even missed Helen. It's not that at all. Hawk made it clear he wanted me to leave. He's not looking to give me a job."

Little wrinkles appeared around his eyes as he leaned forward again, the thoughts all jumbled up and spelled out on his expression.

He shook his head for a few seconds before the words came. "Hawk might say that he doesn't want you here, but I don't think it's true. He hasn't been the same man since you left. I'll talk to him. He might be saying that, but I know him well enough to know it's not what—"

"No, Zab. You're not getting it. He was ready to drag me into a puddle to get me back to Salem tonight. When I left a couple months ago, he rushed me out the door, didn't even give me a chance to say goodbye to you in person."

One of Zab's most endearing qualities was his loyalty. Right now, one of Zab's most frustrating qualities was his loyalty. His inability to believe anything bad of the people he was close to was almost insurmountable. Hawk's slight was still fresh and stinging. I had zero desire to convince Zab of how little Hawk wanted me around when I didn't particularly like to think about it myself.

"Ah, shit. Does that mean you're going back?" He looked like a kid who'd just been told he was getting no birthday gifts.

"No. I'm staying, whether Hawk wants me to or not." Here was the moment of truth. Would he tell me to leave or would he try to help me make it here, when I so desperately needed any friend I could get?

I had to wait for the shock of my statement to fully absorb. Hawk wasn't the only person here who thought he owned Xest. A lot of people seemed to think he did. Not to mention the caste system here. It was probably hard for anyone of lower magic to contemplate going against someone as strong as Hawk.

"Good for you! This place is better with you here. And you know I'll help you any way I can."

I hadn't known if he'd go against Hawk, but hearing him say he would? Every nerve that felt like it had been tied up into knots felt like it had just gotten unraveled. Half the battle felt won. I rested an arm on the back of the couch, sagging a little into it.

"Zab, you don't know how good it is to hear that. Could you help me transfer my money back to Xest coin?"

And boom, his eyes were crinkling again and the smile was fading.

"Yeah, well, as much as I want to help, that might be a problem. It's kind of like the mail situation. You can send money over, but you can't send any back."

I lost a little of my looseness. It wasn't the end of the

world. I'd been penniless before and wasn't a stranger to pulling myself up. I'd always planned on getting a job here. The timeline would simply be moved up.

"I can spot you some cash? It's not a problem."

"Are you sure? I don't want to put you in a spot."

"You won't be. I don't even know what to spend half my money on anyway. It's just sitting around piling up. It'll be good to put it to some use."

"I'll pay you back. I just need a couple of dollars so I can get a hotel room and a few things to tide me over until I find a job."

He cringed enough to show teeth. Oh no. Another problem.

"We don't have hotels here."

"None? Not even someone who rents out a room occasionally?" I'd been holding out hope, even though I'd never see one myself.

"The people who are here all live here. I could help you find a place to rent if you want? Give you a reference if you need, and you can crash on my couch for a bit. It'll be fun."

Now not only would I have to borrow Zab's coin, it looked like I'd be borrowing his apartment. Maybe I should've gone back to Salem until I had this planned out a little better. But how would I ever get back? I'd grabbed the only opportunity I'd had, and another might never come around.

"I don't know. I thought I was going to come here and ask for a small favor. Not make you save me utterly and completely."

Zab was already off the couch and digging through a trunk as he said, "Who saved me from a dragon?"

"A dragon that was there because of me."

"Maybe, but it wasn't going to turn down a tasty treat, and I take good care of myself. There's no way I wouldn't be tasty." He turned around with an armful of blankets and pillows.

"Could I make a place to stay?" I asked as I watched him dump his bedding on the couch next to me.

He shook his head with the gravity of a two-ton weight. "You're strong, but making a place to live when you don't know what you're doing can be pretty danger-ous. If you don't have the skill down, it can disappear when you're in it and kill you. It's happened before."

"I just figured…"

"You can't judge what can be done by what Hawk does or did. No, you'll stay here until we find you a place. It'll be fun."

3

I'd barely gotten my eyes open when Zab walked over and pointed to a bag of my old clothes sitting beside the couch.

"Look what I found," Zab said, smiling like he'd performed a miracle.

I yawned and stretched, while trying to impart some enthusiasm into my tone. "Wow, all my old things. That's...amazing."

"Yeah, I figured you'd feel better having them, since you came over without a chance to pack," he said as he made his way to his stove.

He came back over, handing me tea and a piece of toast made from black bread. I still didn't know what that bread was exactly, but I'd been dreaming of its sour taste for months.

"Thanks. I'm going to start looking for a job today. I don't want you to worry that I'm going to be a drain on you forever." I dug through the bag, looking for a couple of the better pieces I'd left behind. The things I had acquired in Xest before I left hadn't really fit the dress code back in Salem.

"I'm sure you'll find something fast. Everyone knows how strong you are. They'd be crazy not to hire you. Well, I'll be off to the broker house. I set the door so you can get back in."

"Thanks, Zab." I gave him a wave before he disappeared, hoping he was right. The way I'd left here, with the wall I'd created in the Unsettled Lands around it, I wasn't sure if I was going to be a hero or a villain in Xest.

I stepped out onto the streets half an hour later, feeling invigorated. I'd put together a decent outfit of black pants and a slightly funky blue sweater that did some nice things for my figure and looked job-presentable. My old necklace, the one I'd still worn even back in Salem, was sitting on the table near Zab's couch. This was going to be the first day of my new life, one where I didn't hide in the shadows and pretend I was something I wasn't.

To add to that, a man walking down the street nodded in my direction before elbowing his friend, who then did the same. Well, that was a nice indication of things to come. I'd gotten off to a rough start yesterday, but today was a brand-new day.

I walked another few feet and encountered a couple. They both noticed me at the same time. They sneered and crossed the street, saying something about a "Nowhere witch." What the hell was that? Was it a different type of witch? Like a Whimsy? Or Middling? Asking them wasn't possible unless I wanted to chase them down the street.

Another handful of people passed by, and a very clear pattern was emerging: respectful nods, or sneers and eye daggers. There was definitely another "Nowhere witch" muttered again, too. Once might've been a mistake. Growing up with the mother I had, living a life where things always seemed a little off, it was hard to shake off all that bred-in paranoia. Twice? No. I definitely wasn't hearing things.

The other thing that I wasn't imagining was everyone knew who I was. I'd expected some of them to know me, but not *all* of them. I'd never met most of these people. They must've been passing pictures around. Even if I did get a little stage fright, there would be no more hiding in the shadows, not here, not after what I'd done before I left, leaving a monstrosity of a wall in the middle of the Unsettled Lands.

There had been a clear divide over the *thing* out there, and now I seemed to be an extension of that. If they got the warm fuzzies from the lurking entity in the forest, they hated me. If they felt the way I did, like it was the guard dog to hell, where you would rot in despair for the rest of your years, they had a newfound respect for me. Or maybe just a touch of civility, but I'd take it over the sneers.

I pushed all the nods and sneers out of my head as I neared my first stop, the Sweet Shop, and not for a cocoa. I'd have to watch every coin until I landed myself a job. I'd had a decent relationship with the owner, Gilli, and working in a candy shop? There were worse things.

I walked past the broker building, trying to not look but not obviously looking away either. It was a tough balance to achieve. Musso was probably inside, and probably knew from Zab that I was back. How did I walk past and not say hello?

Dammit. I crossed the street and saw his scruffy, bent

head. I knocked on the glass to catch his attention and gave him a wave and a smile when he looked up. He held up a finger, telling me to wait, but not waving me in.

Musso was a slick old guy. He'd already figured out why I wasn't coming in.

I waited a few steps away, hoping Hawk wouldn't happen past.

Musso strode out like a long-lost uncle, except one I couldn't hug. I'd never been a hugger before, but now the lack of them was making me miss them sorely.

I got one of his rare smiles. "How are you, kid? Zab told me you were back."

"I'm doing good. How about you?"

"Come on, walk with me and I'll buy you a cocoa," he said, heading across the street.

I fell into step beside him without the slightest hesitation, like everything was just as it had been. So easy, and yet nothing was the same.

"I know Hawk might be looking to give you a hard time, but you stand strong," he said.

"Zab told you all of it?"

"Didn't have to. I've been around a long time," he said as he paused outside the Sweet Shop.

"Hawk could've done worse. I said I wasn't going back, and he left it alone." All in all, it hadn't gone that bad.

Musso smiled a little and nodded. He wasn't really agreeing or disagreeing.

"I really laid out my feelings, and maybe for once he took it to heart. I was quite firm," I continued.

He was still giving me those ambiguous nods that made me want to look over my shoulder to see what I was missing.

"Do you think I've got a problem?" I asked.

"Not necessarily a problem, but I'd be ready to stand my ground. That's all."

Oh, I was definitely going to do that. Musso hadn't heard what I'd said to Hawk. I wasn't the same person who had come here the first time. I wasn't rolling over for anyone. Even if Hawk was going to be stubborn, let him try. It wasn't like he owned all of Xest.

We walked into the Sweet Shop, and Gilli waved to greet me over the counter. "Wait right there. I'm bringing you a cocoa myself," she called out.

Musso nodded to the door. "I've got some appointments coming in, but if you need anything, you come tell me, okay? He's been gone most mornings anyway."

"I will."

Musso left, and I watched as he crossed the street, heading back to the broker's office. I would go back there, but only to visit, right after I got a job and a place to call my own. I'd march in and show Hawk I was in Xest for good and making a success of it. He wasn't running me out of anywhere.

But first I had to get the job and a place to live.

"Heard you went back. Are you here for good?" Gilli asked as she walked toward me with the cocoa.

"I am. That's one of the reasons I stopped by." This place was always busy. Surely she must hire every so often.

Even as we were talking, she was fixing one of the candy displays.

"Oh? Can I help out somehow?" she asked.

One of her employees walked over, refilling the barrels along the wall beside us. Definitely really busy, and she sure looked like they could use some help.

"Actually, I was looking for a job. I just got back, and

Hawk doesn't need me over at the broker house. I was wondering if you might need any help around here?"

Gilli's mouth was gaping open, and it was very clear what the answer would be when she did get around to speaking.

Her employee glanced over. "Oh, that's gre—"

Gilli's employee didn't get a chance to finish.

"I just hired someone yesterday," Gilli said, finding her words.

"You did?" the employee asked.

"Yes," Gilli said, nodding. "He's going to start next week. I would've swiped you up in a second if I'd known."

The employee was staring at Gilli, and then at the ceiling, as if trying to remember something. The furrow on her forehead might as well have been shaped like a question mark before her mouth turned into an O.

"It's fine. Not a big deal. Thanks anyway. And thanks for the cocoa. I just love this place, so I thought I'd stop here first and see." It was all true. I did love this place, or had. Right now, I was feeling like I'd just found out the boy I was crushing on, who I'd thought was crushing on me back, thought I was frumpy and smelled.

Gilli looked to me and then her employee before looking back at me, as if at a loss for words. The situation had gone from optimistic, to awkward, to one of those dreams where you lost your pants and everyone was staring at you. Since her employee was afraid to talk, and Gilli was struggling with words as well, I was left to fill the growing stretch of silence as we stared uncomfortably at each other.

I took a step back. "But like I said, it's not a big deal. I've got a long list of places I'm going to stop in."

Something about that last bit made her look like I'd just slammed her fingers in a car door.

"Okay, so I really have to get going. Busy day ahead of me."

Gilli forced a smile. I forced one back and then got out of there. At least I had a cocoa to soothe the hurt a bit. She hadn't wanted me, and she clearly needed *someone*. Was it my reputation? The wall? The dragon incident? The grouslies? What had I done so wrong that I'd scared her off?

It didn't matter. There were plenty of other places to work in Xest, and one of them would be looking for help —and maybe desperate enough to hire me.

The butcher shop next. I'd never met them, or had anything to do with them. Maybe they wouldn't know who I was. Maybe they hadn't seen whatever picture or billboard that had my face plastered on it.

Swinging the door open with confidence, I was immediately greeted with a sneer from the man behind the counter. I didn't bother saying a word before turning around and leaving. Definitely a nonstarter.

The next stop was the Stationery and Sundries. The owner there had been a nosy sort, but his weird cat-bird had liked me. Maybe he'd be of the nodding variety? I needed some nodding shop owners right now.

I walked in, and the older man who owned the shop lifted his head, giving me a slight nod. "I heard you were back."

No sneer. It was safe.

"Yep, it's me. I'm back." Bassy, his cat-bird pet, leapt onto the shelf next to my shoulder, purred loudly, and began butting his head up against me.

"So, what can I do for you?" His eyes were taking in his

cat-bird and then me, as if I were hypnotizing the thing or something.

Could I really work for him? Was I desperate enough to have him eyeing me up all day long? It wasn't as if he'd leave me be. He'd grill me from morning to night. He'd want to know everything I was doing. That's the type he was. I remembered clearly how he'd questioned me the first time I came here, his stare thick with suspicion, and that was before everything that had happened.

Although he wasn't grilling me yet.

And yes, I was that desperate.

"I was wondering if you could use some help around here? Or maybe a..." Couldn't call Bassy a cat. That might be insulting. Not a good way to ask for a job. "A sitter?"

"No, I'm just a one-man show. Never had any help and don't need it now," he said as he continued staring at me as if I'd cast a spell on him.

"Well, if you change your mind, you can always send me a newsflash."

He nodded, this one half as friendly as the last. Time to make my exit. Bassy was about to leap onto my shoulders if I didn't get out of there soon.

The restaurant Hawk had brought me to was next. I knew they didn't like me, but it was right here, and I was going to stop everywhere. I couldn't be sure if they'd sneer until I tried.

One step inside and a roomful of sneers met me. I turned right around. Even if the owner would hire me, that might've been a little too hostile an environment to handle.

I crossed the street to the shop I'd bought Rabbit an outfit in on her last day in Xest, hoping there might be some goodwill.

The store owner nodded at me. "Can I help you? Are you looking for anything in particular?"

"I was wondering if you were looking for a sales clerk or had any positions open?"

Her lips parted as her eyes darted to the door before returning to me. I could see right where this was headed and was determined to turn this ship around. Was it because I was an outsider?

"Just so you know, I have a lot of experience in sales. I worked in a shop for years and was always on time and extremely responsible. I can provide a reference as well."

She swallowed, then stared at the door again and back to me.

"That's very nice," she said, straightening things on the counter. "But I'm not hiring right now. Try back in a year or so. Maybe things will have changed by then."

I took a step toward her, fed up with all the twitchy shop owners who never needed help even when they appeared completely understaffed. "Was it the wall? It's clearly something."

"No, not at all. I'm sorry. I just don't need anyone," she said. "I would've loved to hire you."

I forced a smile and a wave as I left. *Loved to?* If she'd really loved to, she could've. She had piles along the wall that she clearly didn't have time to get to.

Didn't matter. There were plenty more places in Xest. Someone would hire me.

4

No one was going to hire me. There were no more places in Xest I could think to try. I'd been to every open business I could find that would let me in the door. Now the sun was setting and I was no better off than I had been this morning. Hawk did own this place, and he was doing a mighty good job of making it hard to stay.

I'd been wrong, so utterly wrong that if this had been a graded test, I wouldn't have even gotten five percent correct. Still, I wasn't giving up. It would take a lot more than this to make me quit.

The old, rusty mailbox was the final stop of the day. I'd drop off my letter to Rabbit, letting her know I'd ended up back in Xest, so she didn't worry. I'd written it to her last night, so it read a little more optimistic than my current state of mind. If I'd had to write something now, it might've been closer to "see you in a few days."

Heading back to Zab's, I drew a mental map of Xest, wondering if I'd overlooked a place. There had to be other places hiring here. Zab would know. If he didn't, Musso might. He might have a connection that would help me get a foot in the door. It wasn't like I was aiming high. I'd take anything. Hand me a broom or a mop as long as it came with a paycheck. Scrubbing dishes, digging ditches, whatever it took.

A man came close enough to me that I jumped back before he accidentally hit me.

"Go away, Nowhere witch," he said as he passed by.

Great. I'd moved beyond sneers to getting run off the street? It was the last slight of the day, and one too many.

"What did you say to me?" I didn't realize how loud I was until a few people across the street stopped in their tracks to see what was going down.

He stopped and turned back toward me. "I said, *go away,* Nowhere witch."

Whatever a Nowhere witch was, the way he said the words made it sound like it was the lowest of the low. Be nice to know what it meant so I knew how to respond. I'd have to take a leap and just run with it.

"I'm not going *anywhere.*"

"We'll see about that," he said. A few stragglers were gathered behind him, all sneering in my direction, as if they'd been waiting for a moment like this to gang up.

Great. Now he had a group. Still, I wasn't backing down.

"Oh yes, we will see." I still couldn't defend myself worth a damn with magic, but if he pushed me too far, called my bluff, I wasn't above punching him in the face. I might be on the small side, but I was strong and scrappy. Hopefully the rest of them wouldn't jump me.

My offender was suddenly at a loss for words as he looked over my shoulder. With a last sneer in my direction, he walked away, his little group dispersing with him.

I should've been relieved I had backup too, but this

wasn't how I wanted to end my day. There was one person who could clear the street, and I'd already had enough humiliation. I didn't need Hawk as an audience, saving the damsel who'd be better off in Salem.

"I didn't need your help. I had it covered." I spun and found a tall, dark-haired man standing there, but not Hawk. Oscar, who was still smiling in spite of my tone, appeared to be the man who'd come to my defense this time. I was just going to alienate everyone today, wasn't I?

"Excuse me for helping out a friend," Oscar replied, his soft hazel eyes gleaming.

I gave him a humbled half-smile. "I'm sorry. I thought you were..." I threw up my hands. I probably didn't have to spell it out to one of Hawk's friends.

"Understandable, given the situation," he said, laughing.

Oscar had the kind of laugh that came often and easy. I could use a little of his levity right now, but that didn't mean he wasn't here to reinforce the troops.

"Are you going to try to run me out, too?"

"He's my friend, but he's also an asshole, and this is coming from someone who's held that title enough to be a reigning champ. But no, I'm not taking sides in this fight." He took a step away from me but waved a hand, motioning for me to follow. "Come on, you look like you've had a rough day. Let me buy you a drink."

"I don't know. I kind of just wanted to—"

"Head to Zab's and crawl into a ball and cry? I think my offer is better, at least by a little bit, don't you?" He held up his fingers, leaving the slightest bit of air between them.

I started walking. "Fine. But just so you know, I wasn't going to cry. I was going to crawl into a ball and have tea, thank you very much." I had a rule against crying, and it wouldn't be broken because of one bad day filled with a lot of sneers and refusals.

"That's only because you don't cry," he said, looking at me like he *knew* things. "But if you were the type to cry, it would be game on right now."

It was unclear whether he was trying to tease me out of a bad mood or just amuse himself. Either way, it was working, so I'd take it.

"How do you know I don't cry?" I asked. No matter how he wanted to portray it, he didn't know things. We'd never been that close, and I was a closed book. I kept it that way until I was sure you weren't the type of person who dog-eared the pages or broke the spine. I'd taken too many dings to let just anyone flip my pages about.

"I was there after one of your attacks, remember? You know, the whole..." He put his hands to his throat and made a choking noise.

Oh yes, what a nice reenactment of the night an invisible monster nearly choked me to death. Clearly, there was nothing off the table when it came to Oscar's personal amusement.

"How could I forget with such a glorious reminder?" I asked.

"If you weren't all weepy-eyed after that one, pretty good odds you don't cry easily."

Maybe he did know a few things. He was definitely observant.

The longer we walked, two things became very apparent. One, Oscar didn't have that annoying habit of Hawk's, where he'd be a few feet ahead of me. At least Hawk hadn't corrupted his friend in that way. Two, just like Hawk, people cleared the street for Oscar. It wasn't quite the same "make a break for it" kind of berth, but there was definitely an area of magical respect, you might call it. Or maybe plain old fear, because when I looked around, the nods were still coming but the sneers had stopped almost completely. Now I had to decipher friend from foe by impartiality. It was an improvement. I was a tough girl, as Oscar had implied, but I wasn't made of steel. I'd taken enough dirty looks to fill my glass ten times over today.

"Hey, do you know what a Nowhere witch is? I've never heard of it. Is that a different name for Whimsy witch or something?"

There was a heavy lag before he answered. "You already heard about that, huh? Guess it's not a surprise."

"What's it mean?"

"I'll tell you, but only because you're not a crier, so don't prove me wrong." He glanced at me, seeking confirmation he wouldn't have a bawling mess on his hands.

"Like you said, I don't cry. Now tell me."

"It's what people call witches who don't belong anywhere. You've got no home. You've got nowhere. Typically it's been reserved for witches who don't have any magic left because they can't stay in Xest any longer."

Whoa. That one hit a nerve. I hadn't thought anything he could say would make me actually *want* to cry, so why were my eyes burning? I wasn't going to go back on my word, but this was a little tougher than I'd thought. I might still have magic, not that I'd been using it, but I didn't have a home. I was straddling two worlds right now and didn't seem to belong in either.

"Hey, you're not getting funny on me, right?" Oscar asked, watching me as if he sensed the little swarm of bees attacking my eyes.

"Not at all. Just curious why they would call me that." I

rubbed the back of my hand across my nose while clearing my throat.

"Maybe they think you won't last long after that wall you made in the Unsettled Lands. They probably think you're nearly used up." Oscar shrugged, as if he didn't think that would be a problem.

I tripped but caught myself fast enough that I didn't need any help staying on my feet. What if they were right? What if I didn't have much magic left? I hadn't even tested out my magic in months, if you didn't count *accidentally* jumping into every puddle I'd seen. That hadn't worked before I left Xest, so I hadn't worried about it not working then, too.

But *shit*. What if I had fought to get back here and I was running on fumes?

"Hey, you're tough, remember?" Oscar reminded me.

"I'm fine." I was, or would be soon.

"Okay, well, you better be. If you let what those losers said get to you, I'm going to have to rethink my opinion. I don't like that many people, and I was just on the brink of thinking you might be okay, but if you let some ass take you down that easy, I might be wrong."

He might've still been talking, but there were more important matters. Could I still do magic? Had I run out? Rabbit had told me that most witches did. Why would I be different?

"Tippi, what are you doing?" Oscar asked, his voice firm and loud.

"Oh, nothing," I said, tucking my hand back in my pocket. This wasn't the time to experiment.

"You didn't run out," he said.

He might know some things, and he might be perceptive, but that had been an easy one.

"How do you know?"

"Because that wall would've wiped out nearly anyone who wasn't an infinite. The fact that you're standing here breathing tells me you still have magic, but if you'd like me to confirm it..."

He grabbed my wrist and yanked off my glove, wrapping his hand around mine. The sizzle of magic intermingling was instant.

He dropped my hand. "You're fine. More than fine. You might have more than is good for you." He handed me back my glove while shaking his head. "I *knew* he was underplaying it," Oscar said, more to himself than me.

"What are you talking about?" I asked, clasping my hands together, wishing there were some way to self-test.

"Ask Hawk." He laughed, leaving me wondering while he opened the door.

I looked up, realizing we'd stopped in front of a building with darkened windows and no sign. It was a bar of sorts. Hawk had brought me here what seemed like ages ago to meet some of his people. It was the only place I hadn't begged for a job in today, mostly because it didn't look like it was open for customers, or people that hadn't been stamped and approved by Hawk.

The place was dimly lit, with a scattering of candles around the room and a smoky haze that seemed to be a permanent fixture in the place.

There were only a handful of people inside. A couple of guys sitting in the corner that looked up as we walked in, who nodded in our direction, and a man wiping down the bar. He had a face that looked like it had been dried and tanned a thousand years ago, black hair pulled back, adding to the severity of his expression.

Oscar grabbed a stool, and I took the one beside him.

"Oscar, what can I get you two tonight?" the barman asked as he gave me a once-over.

"Zark, I'll have an ale, and something hot for my friend here."

Boiling sounded good right about now. I wasn't sure anything else would remove the permafrost from my limbs.

"How about a smokin' mordi?" Zark asked me.

"It's like a hot toddy in Rest," Oscar said.

"That would be wonderful," I replied.

"And a couple of those buttered buns you always have stashed in back."

Buttered buns? This was definitely better than being curled up in the corner of Zab's couch.

"How many places did you try to get hired at today?" Oscar asked.

"All of them. Every place I could find," I answered, and didn't even mind. My attention was on the plate of buns heading our way. They looked like some sort of cinnamon bun, dripping in butter.

The steaming drink Zark placed next to it smelled like heaven and tasted even better. I'd had a hot toddy before, but this tasted more like melted caramel.

I was halfway through a bun when Oscar turned to Zark and asked, "Hey, weren't you looking for some help around here?"

I sipped on the smokin' mordi, trying to get that last bite down while I nudged Oscar with my boot under the bar. Zark wasn't going to hire me, and I was hoping to have a relaxing drink without a side of humiliation.

"I'm always hiring on and off, but not right now," he said, his eyes darting in my direction and then back to

Oscar, sending a signal that could've been shot off by a flare gun.

Yep. As expected. Too bad the reason wasn't as apparent. Was it because I was from Rest? Did they think I was incapable of doing hard work? Or did they think all Resters were stupid? If I just knew the reason...

"But word was you *are* looking for some help," Oscar said, as if I hadn't kicked him.

I kicked him again, harder this time.

"I haven't seen any new help," Oscar said.

Did Oscar have feeling in his shins?

"Oscar, let it go. He knows who I am and he doesn't want me." I stared at the half-eaten bun. It didn't taste anywhere near as good as I'd thought a few moments ago. Actually, he'd clearly over-buttered it, which I hadn't thought possible. I'd take the rest back to Zab's. Maybe they had a to-go cup for the smokin' mordi? There was a good chance both would taste better again once I got the hell out of here.

"Everyone knows who you are," Zark said to me before turning back to Oscar. "I just can't do it."

I gave a short nod. I really should've followed my gut and gone back to Zab's. Although I wasn't completely empty-handed. I took the bun and put it on a napkin to wrap up for later. I'd have to leave the smokin' mordi behind.

"I think you can," Oscar said, with a serious tone that was at complete odds with his earlier playfulness.

"Oscar, he doesn't want to hire me. Leave it be. If he doesn't want me, I don't want the job." And I didn't want to eat here either. But I'd eat his bun somewhere else. I put it in my pocket as I got up from the stool.

Zark was shaking his head and holding up his hand.

"Now hang on a second. It's not that I don't want to hire you. You did us a solid over in the Unsettled Lands with the wall. It's just—"

"I'll take the heat for it," Oscar said.

Why would there be any heat with hiring me? I sat back down, watching the expressions warring on Zark's face as he and Oscar were about to square off. Zark might've wanted to hire me. I was afraid to say anything that would stop this from unfolding. What was going on here?

"It's on you? You're vouching?" Zark asked Oscar.

"Yes. That's what I just said." Oscar stared squarely back at him.

Zark turned back to me. "Then you've got yourself a job. Be here tomorrow afternoon."

"Are you saying you'll hire me?" I asked, not believing what I was hearing.

"I'm pretty sure that's what I'm saying. If Oscar here is willing to shoulder the heat, I'd be happy to. We owe you a debt."

"Shoulder the heat for what? Why is there any heat involved with hiring me?" He'd just said it wasn't the wall, so what was the issue?

"Hawk is trying to run you out of Xest," Zark said.

"You mean no one will hire me because of Hawk?" My blood was simmering at the mere possibility.

"Of course that's what I mean. Even the people who don't like him don't want to cross him." Zark was frowning at me, as if he doubted my intelligence for asking such a question.

I jerked back as if I'd been punched. It sure felt that way right now. "Is Hawk telling people not to hire me?"

Zark waved his hand in the air, shaking his head. "It

doesn't work like that here. Everyone knows he wants you out. Doesn't need to be said."

I turned to Oscar. He didn't confirm, but the shrug was enough to imply that it was his take too. Then there had been Musso earlier, trying to tell me to "stand my ground." He'd suspected I'd have a problem as well.

All the elation and excitement of getting a job two seconds ago deflated, like my celebration balloons had a run-in with a sticker bush. Had Hawk really done that? Did he want me gone so bad that he'd bar me from making a living? Being able to put a roof over my head and eat? Trying to have an honest go at a life in Xest?

How was it possible to like someone, feel such loyalty to them, and then hate them so very much?

Zark took another glance at me and then suddenly had some other things to handle in the back.

"Hey, at least you still have a shit-ton of magic," Oscar said, smiling and pointing to my drink. My smokin' mordi, which had been losing its steam before, was boiling over the glass. Shit.

I took the napkins and tried to stem the eruption.

"Am I doing that?"

"Just take a couple deep breaths and hold them. It won't stop until you calm down."

I did as he said, and as he'd predicted, the drink stopped bubbling.

"That's never happened before," I said as I tried to sop up the mess around the glass.

"It's normal. Usually happens at a younger age, but considering your history..." I must've looked stumped, because he continued. "Your magical muscles are growing, and you still don't really have any practice controlling them."

"At least it's hot again," I said, then took a sip as I eyed up Oscar.

The first time I met him was when he'd brought the magic tester gem to Hawk, and his arrogance and glib remarks had runneth over. Turned out he was a pretty nice guy. Maybe nicer than I even realized.

"You didn't just run into me on the street today, did you? You came to find me. You knew what Hawk was up to." I narrowed my eyes at him.

"I still don't know if this was his plan or a happy happenstance for him, but I suspected you'd have an issue."

"Your friend is a jerk."

"Like I said, he can be." Oscar spread his hands in a *what can you do* gesture.

"Thanks, Oscar. You really helped me out." It sucked that hugs weren't acceptable in Xest.

He shook his head. "Don't go laying that halo on my head anytime soon. I have my own reasons."

"What would your reasons be to get me a job?" My desire to hug him was diminishing.

He leaned back in his seat with his drink, a small smile on his lips. "I have them. Don't worry, though—no debt to be paid, at least not from you."

5

I'd been avoiding the broker's office, more specifically, the owner of the brokerage. Now I barged in, hoping to find Hawk here. The place was closed, but the door still opened for me, which meant he hadn't revoked my key. How nice of him to allow me easy access here, considering he was trying to have me run out of Xest.

The main office was empty, and so was the back room. The door upstairs wouldn't open to his place unless he wanted it that way, which he wouldn't. I could leave him a note, but a scathing memo didn't pack the same punch as a good old rant in person.

There was a pile of newsflash papers on Zab's desk. That would certainly get him here, but then all of Xest would know my business—or more of it, anyway. There had been enough of it on display today.

I wandered about the room I hadn't set foot in for months. My table was still there, baskets in place, the flower still there as well. Was Zab watering my flower, or had Hawk hired someone else to come and do the sorting and they were tending it? I ignored the urge to throw the table onto its side at the thought. He could do whatever he wanted. Hawk and this place were in my rearview.

The Helexorgomay's gears churned, stopped, and then repeated a little faster. I glanced up at Helen, the wish machine that took up most of the upper wall. Some people found the sound of the ocean, or birds chirping in spring, soothing. Not me. This was the sound I'd missed. It reminded me of a screen door slamming in summer as you walked in your house after a long day, the sound of your family's laughter and the familiar creak of a floorboard.

"It's been a long while," I said, laying a hand on the bronze machinery, feeling the hum of her immense magic as it sent a tingle through my fingers.

Helen's gears picked up speed and then stopped. A little slip of paper flew out of the slot and landed by my feet, face-up.

I told you not to leave. You're supposed to be here.

Did she know why I'd left? The way things had gone down? The way Hawk had rushed me out before I'd gotten a chance to even say proper goodbyes? Probably. She was the great Helexorgomay machine. The all-knowing Helen. She'd know every detail, probably down to the kiss and the angry reaction right afterward. She probably thought I should've been tougher. I had been most of my life, but when I came here, I'd had a blip.

When I came here, not knowing what to do, at a complete loss, I'd trusted Hawk. I'd started to rely on him. I'd let him take control of my life in a way I'd never let anyone before. And when he told me to leave, I'd done it, even if it hadn't felt right. I'd regretted it ever since. I wouldn't fold again, not ever.

I folded the paper and put it in my pocket, wanting a small piece of this place, of her, in case I never set foot in here again. It was a reminder that even if things got tough again, Helen thought I belonged. She was the wish machine. If someone had an opinion I should trust, it was hers.

"I know. I should've fought harder. I will this time, though."

Another slip shot out.

Don't. Fold. Again. You're stronger than you realize.

Fold. She'd used the same word I'd thought of. Yeah, Helen knew it all.

Another slip flew to my feet.

Yes, I do.

"Now you're just showing off," I said, pocketing these slips as well. I might frame one and hang it once I got a place of my own. It was nice that Helen thought I was strong, especially when I was having doubts.

The door opened behind me. There was only one person that would come in here this late. The adrenaline that had been soothed by memories and Helen came roiling back to a full boil as I turned to face Hawk.

He walked into the room with that same arrogance I remembered and sat on Zab's desk, crossing his arms while he stared at me as if he was absolved of all guilt. Or maybe he was incapable of feeling any? One of the first thoughts in my head was that damn, he looked good tonight. It showed how messed up my head was. You didn't admire the devil's attractive facade. It was just honey to lure you to the trap. I'd never fall for his trap again.

"Can I help you with something?"

He was utterly calm, always in control. I hated it even as I longed to emulate it.

"You told everyone not to hire me." I didn't scream or rage the way I'd planned. He didn't deserve that much emotion out of me. I'd play his game, as if I were above it all, even if I felt as if I were covered in mud and muck after the day I'd had.

"I didn't instruct anyone."

Again with the semantics. Did everyone in this place split hairs? Could we not just sum it up nice and simple for once? "You're denying that you were the reason I had trouble getting a job?"

"Not at all. I'm simply informing you that I didn't have to tell them. When you didn't come back to work here, they were wary of how welcome you were. Since I believe you shouldn't be here, did you think I'd go out of my way to have them hire you?" He raised an eyebrow, as if to imply I couldn't possibly be that stupid.

I'd made a huge mistake coming here. I wasn't laying down the law. I was getting tied in knots of aggravation and fury, while he watched on. I was becoming a jumbled-up mess inside while he was a placid lake. I needed to get out of here, and now, before the tsunami inside me raged outward and it became very clear who was holding it together and who was crumbling.

"I'm aware that you think I shouldn't be here. Luckily for me, it doesn't matter what you think anymore, because I will be staying, and someone *did* give me a job. So thank you for trying to screw me, and I'll be on my way."

Some papers behind me fluttered to the floor, and the flower pot was rattling on the desk. That was definitely my signal to exit.

I headed for the door, but he blocked my way. He was a foot in front of me, scanning me the length of me, and not in a sexual way.

"There's something different. I thought I noticed it the other night as well." His eyes rose to mine. "What have you done?"

My hand moved to my neck before I caught myself and held it in front of me. His glance down made it clear he hadn't missed the slip.

Out of everyone, he would be the one to notice. I wasn't even sure if it had done something, but it must've the way he was acting.

"I have no idea what you're talking about. Now step out of my way."

"There's something different," he said, still blocking my path as if I hadn't spoken.

"Yes. *Me.* Now move." Shoving him out of the way was not an option, but only because he was stronger. Otherwise, his ass would've been on the ground.

He didn't budge. I tried to step around him, and he shifted with me, grabbing my wrist and pushing my jacket up so he could feel my flesh, or more specifically, my magic. I was getting a little tired of being handled tonight, although when Oscar had done it, it wasn't quite so unnerving.

Trying to shrug him off did nothing.

"Get off me."

He only moved closer, his head dipping down beside mine as if he were going to whisper in my ear. Instead, he breathed deeply of me.

"You've gotten stronger. But how is that possible?" He wasn't talking to me but thinking aloud. It was so un-Hawk-like that it meant he was truly stumped.

I wasn't. But then again, he'd never known about the tattoo. Or that a couple of specks of ink had remained until recently. I wasn't sure why those last few spots had bothered me. They'd appeared as nothing more than freckles, but I'd fixated on them when I was stuck in Salem, dwelling on what I'd lost, pretending I hadn't cared. I'd obsessed enough to get one more laser treatment done so there wasn't a single reminder of what had been stolen from me.

One hand was still on my wrist as his other threaded through my hair, working its way around to the back of my neck.

"What was here?"

He was skimming over the place that had once had my tattoo. I tried not to shiver from his touch. I'd forgotten how it infused me. Or I'd *tried* to forget, but it was all racing back to me now, making my heart race. The huskiness of his voice hadn't been missed by me either. He felt it too, even now as he tried to concentrate on this other mystery.

"You were marked. Was it your mother? I can still feel the trace of its energy."

I tried pushing away and ended up flattened against him.

"Do you have no boundaries?" I asked as he fixated on my skin and there wasn't much I could do about it. One hand still had my wrist while the other was pressed on my neck.

"Of course it was her. Who else?"

I didn't answer. It was none of his business. The only thing that kept me standing there was that I refused to struggle further.

His fingers continued to graze over the area, and heat built up along my skin.

"What are you doing?"

He kept going, repeating a word I didn't understand, as my skin grew hotter by the second. His fingers kept moving over the spot until it was near burning.

I'd never thought he'd actually hurt me, but the more the heat grew, the more I doubted my beliefs. I pushed against him, harder than even before. He pressed me back to him, continuing with whatever it was he was doing.

Then, finally, the heat faded. His hands stopped and he stepped away from me. He walked across the room, as if he were the one looking for space.

My hand went to the spot that still burned and tingled with his magic.

"What the hell was that? What did you do to me?" I asked as I moved even farther away from him, in the direction of the door. If he'd put something back there, I'd kill him right now. Somehow, I'd manage.

He leaned on a desk, looking at me, and he didn't look like the placid lake anymore. His waters had been riled as well, and I was seeing some waves about to break along the rock, if I read him right.

"There was still a little of the magic blocker left. I got rid of it for you."

Bullshit. Why would he do that for me? Why help me in any way?

I stretched my shoulders and rolled my neck, feeling the area out for something wrong. As much as I didn't trust him, it did feel a little looser, like I'd gotten a shoulder massage or something. My entire life, I'd always had a tightness around my neck that had eased of late, but now it was completely gone.

"Why didn't you ask me?" I rolled my neck a bit more. Had he really gotten rid of it completely? I hadn't felt this loose in more than a decade, probably right around the time... Yeah, he really might've.

"You would've let me? You didn't trust me enough to tell me it was there in the first place."

Oh, those waves were definitely crashing now. I wasn't sure what had unraveled him, but he was right on my level now, and I liked it.

Sort of. The both of us unraveled might not be a good thing.

Either way, he was right. No way would I have let him touch a hair on my head at this point. Half of me wanted to thank him, but the other part was still annoyed he'd forced it on me. I nodded. That was as good as I had at the moment, especially since he was trying to run me out of town. Two minutes of beneficial magic wasn't making up for that. Now it was time to get the hell out of there.

I marched out of the office and, for the first time, barely felt the freezing cold of the fifth wind.

6

The square was quieter than usual for this time of night. It had only been a few months, but there was a heaviness in the air that I hadn't remembered. The people who were out looked every which way around them, took a few steps, and then repeated, as if there was an attack imminent. Or maybe it was me, hot off my confrontation with Hawk, expecting a fight. If I did want another one, my opportunity was up ahead.

There was a warm light coming from Raydam's house. I could've spent an extra few minutes walking the other way and avoiding it, but then, I wasn't that girl anymore, right? So I would keep going straight ahead. I was going to start this new life the way I intended on living it, and that was with a head held high, not shrinking from anyone.

He was on the porch, with another figure beside him. The warm light filtering through the window caught his companion's red locks, making them shimmer while outlining her perfect figure.

Raydam and me were on opposite sides, but deep

down, I didn't have any overwhelming vitriol for him. That couldn't be said for Belinda. We hadn't been friends. We'd barely tolerated each other as coworkers, but did that excuse what she'd done? Laying that ill charm to trap me so *it* could get me? Those were war actions, and they wouldn't be soon forgotten. She'd tried to get me out of the way by killing me, as if it were my fault that Hawk hadn't wanted her.

Jilted by Hawk, Belinda had shifted sideways and a bit downhill to the next warm body she could find. It was an all-too-obvious move. Did Raydam know she'd been dumped, or did she spin that little tale in her favor? Did she think this would make Hawk come running back? Maybe he would, and what did I care?

Actually, seemed I did care a bit from the burn in my chest. I'd have to work on that.

I'd figure that out tomorrow. Right now, I had to keep an eye on Raydam, who was clocking my pace. Make that two of them, if I didn't count the people who might be inside his house, and one of me. Screw it. I still wasn't crossing the street. I didn't turn my head and pretend not to see them, either. I stared right at them.

Raydam took a step in my direction, and then another, until he was walking toward me, with Belinda right behind him. I stopped, waiting for him. After all, I didn't run anymore. I shoved my hands in my pockets to show how little they concerned me.

He stopped a few feet shy of me, and then Belinda sidled up to him, staring at me as if I were the one who'd betrayed her.

I stood in silence, my narrowed eyes saying it all.

"I'd heard the Nowhere witch was back," Belinda said. "Apparently not even Hawk wants you now."

"As opposed to Hawk having never wanted me?" I asked, my insult clear enough if her rising chest and quick intake of breath meant anything.

Raydam moved his eyes to her for a moment, the wheels turning. Yes, he'd thought he'd been first choice, not the only one left. Guess again. He'd never be picked first if Hawk were available, not as a friend, partner, lover, not even in a game of dodgeball. Whether I liked Hawk or hated him, I wasn't deluded enough to see that happening. There was hate and then there was stupid. If you let hate run wild enough, it could clog up your brain with gunk that made you stop seeing the world for what it was. In this world, Hawk trumped Raydam every single time.

Raydam finally looked back to me, shrugging off his revelation about Belinda, or not—time would tell, pouring through the hourglass until nothing was left but the ugly truth.

"What's your purpose here? Why are you back in Xest? You've already caused enough damage," Raydam finally said.

"I'm not here for you or your business. I'm here to live my life, like everyone else." There you go. It was about as good of an olive branch as I could muster. The way I saw it, I had enough issues. I wasn't going to run from a fight, but that didn't mean I'd throw the gauntlet at every opponent I could find, either. Now, if Belinda wanted a fight, that would be an entirely different scenario, but it would have to wait a bit.

"You think you can do that after the monstrosity you erected in the Unsettled Lands? You're wrong. You better go back to whatever hellhole you climbed out of and beg them to keep you, because you're not welcome here."

There was running and then there was standing here and listening to this crap.

"As pleasant as this little visit was, I'd best be going. Have a full day planned tomorrow." I turned and walked away, not running. This day had been way too long to use up the last of my energy on Raydam and his crazy new girlfriend.

"Tippi, if you stay, don't say you weren't warned. We will come for you."

"Duly warned," I said, voice full of bravado even as a slight chill snaked up my spine. Just what I needed: more enemies.

As mentioned, I didn't run anymore. But I might walk a little faster on occasion. This day couldn't handle any more confrontations.

I didn't completely unwind until I shut the door to Zab's place.

"How'd it go?" Zab asked as I walked in.

His smile was so forced that I was surprised he wasn't using two fingers on either side of his mouth to prop it up. He'd also started making second-rate cocoa as soon as I walked in, as if he'd known I'd need the pick-me-up. It was a strong switch from his earlier optimism.

"Obviously you heard," I said as I dropped onto the couch. It wasn't a surprise when Xest was so small and I'd hit up every business there was, only to be booted repeatedly.

"Hard not to." His smile slipped until it was a landslide across his face. It dropped so much I was surprised his nose hung in there.

"Well, you heard wrong," I said, smiling as my voice rose. "In spite of Hawk, I got a job over at that club, the one with no name? Zark hired me!" I did a little dance in my seat because my legs were too tired to stand.

"He did?" Zab did a little dance too.

"Yes!"

7

Zark's place was packed the next afternoon. There wasn't a free seat in the joint, and all eyes were on me as I walked in. My nerves would've preferred a slower day, but I sauntered across the room like it was a runway and I a seasoned model.

"Look who's here!" Zark greeted me with a smile that he didn't appear capable of yesterday. He could've been tired the day before, but that wasn't what my gut was telling me. That was another thing I'd decided since I'd come back to Xest: besides not taking any shit and never backing down, the gut ruled the roost. I'd need to establish a pecking order just in case the never backing down conflicted with the gut.

"Yep, I'm here for work, just like you said," I added, in case he needed a reminder he had hired me and I wasn't making a social call.

"Just made a fresh batch of buttered buns. They're in the back. Go grab yourself a couple and have a bite before you start work. I don't want you to get worn down during your shift."

This guy was *really* happy. Were these people all here to see the show? Did they think Hawk was going to march in here and drag me out? Would he try?

"Thank you, but I'm good. I ate before I came." And if I did have an appetite, it was long gone now.

"No, no, I want you to be happy here. Can't have you overtaxing yourself. Now go get that bun, and I'll make you a nice tea to drink with it."

"Okay." He was paying me. If he wanted me to eat a bun that badly, I'd have to eat the bun. They were sitting on a table in the back, still steaming from the oven, as if he'd timed it that way. I put one on a napkin and took it with me back to the bar, where my tea was waiting, along with a very happy Zark.

"You usually this busy?" I asked, guessing it was otherwise.

"Never." His dull eyes twinkled. and his thin lips parted for a crooked smile.

This Zark was even less inviting than the harsh, unhappy version of yesterday. This one looked like we were co-conspirators. This one might want to stuff me and prop my body up in the corner, like some twisted taxidermy display. Zark was also the only one willing to hire me, so he was my best friend for now.

"What should I do?" I asked, throwing more enthusiasm into the question than the gawking crowd instilled.

"I'll show you around the bar," he said, leading the way. "It might take you a while to learn all the drinks, but there's a book right here." He patted a fat leather tome sitting beside a cash box piled halfway up with coin.

"Most of my staff have been high-level Whimsy or low Middling witches and warlocks. I'm guessing this will be easy work for you. Shouldn't even break a sweat."

Magic? This job required the use of magic? I thought I'd be just slinging drinks. I smiled. If he got the impression that meant I agreed with him, at least I hadn't lied. He'd made his own assumption and gauged my reaction accordingly.

A man stepped up to the bar, gave me a nod, and then said to Zark, "Can I get two dragon breaths?"

"We'll bring them right over." Zark grabbed two tall glasses and handed them to me. "Magic-infused drinks are more expensive," he said under his breath. "See those bottles? Put some of the red, a little blue, and a little of that dark green, equal parts in that order."

The colors layered on top of each other as I filled them. This wasn't too bad.

"All good?" I asked.

"Good. Now you just need to infuse them a little. I'll do this one. You watch, and then you do that one." He covered the glass with a little tin, and then shook it and said, "Ardere."

He took off the lid and set the glass down. It had morphed into a lava lamp appearance, with steam rising from the top.

I took the lid, put it on the top of the other drink, and shook it.

"You need to say the word as you do it," Zark said.

I'd already figured that out. I just didn't want to.

"Okay." *Please, let this work out. Let my magic do something smoothly for once. Don't let it go badly.*

He was watching, waiting.

"Ardere," I said as I shook it.

I placed it on the bar as he had, and it looked perfect. It was identical to his lava lamp.

"Knew you'd have no problem," Zark said.

I nodded. Yep. Easy.

"Should I bring them over to the table now?"

"Tell them I'll add them to the tab."

I carried the drinks over and presented them to the two men at the table as if I were presenting them the *Mona Lisa*. It was how I felt about it too. They were both perfect, even mine. It looked every bit as good as Zark's. Hawk could go screw. I belonged here, as a barmaid, a clerk, a whatever. It didn't matter.

Just as I got back to the bar, there was a low growl and then a scream. Then a hush filled the place, along with the smell of burning hair.

Zark, the only one I could see, had his lips parted and his eyes wide open. He hit his forehead before dropping his hand and smothering his face for a moment.

I turned, knowing there was no avoiding the situation. The customer, the one who'd received my drink, was sitting at his table, and his full beard had become stubble.

He stared right at me, perplexed.

"I'm sorry. I'm really sorry."

Zark had finally started moving. He dashed in front of me. "Go wait behind the bar. I'll handle this."

I nodded, doing as I was told.

Zark went over, trying to smooth the customer's feathers as I tried to take in the rest of the customers' reactions. They looked more amused than anything else. Still, I was going to be fired for sure. The only job I could get and I hadn't lasted an hour. It would be all over Xest by tonight. *He'd* know. He'd probably make a special visit to see me and tell me I should go back to Salem. I was sure he'd *known* this was how it would turn out all along.

I stood as far back from the crowd as possible. Maybe they'd forget I was here.

The second Zark walked behind the bar, I said, "I'm so sorry. I really am. I didn't mean for that to happen. I don't know what I did wrong, but I'll do it again, as many times as needed to until I get it right."

He threw up his hands. "No, no, don't do that."

"Then I'm fired?" I looked at the floor, waiting to hear the words. "Of course I'm fired. I blew up your customer's beard. How could I *not* be fired?" *Don't cry, you big ninny. Do not cry. You're not a crier, remember?*

"Now, I wouldn't go as far as firing you."

"You wouldn't?" My head popped right up and my spine straightened like I was a jack-in-the-box.

Zark looked at the crowd, none of whom had left, not even burned-beard guy.

"It wasn't a good showing, but I don't want to be hasty, either. Maybe you do some of the manual stuff and leave the magic to me for now, until you get settled in. It's probably only nerves. There can be magical flare-ups due to nerves." He waved a hand toward the bottles. "But, you know, maybe don't touch too much, and don't do anything magical at all. I mean nothing at all. Don't utter a magical word or have a magical thought, all right?"

The nice Zark was still there, just like all his customers.

"I won't do a thing. Absolutely nothing."

He nodded. "That's good."

"You're going to stay back here with me?" He was hiring me to tend his bar and he couldn't leave? How long would things last like this? "I could maybe just call you if there's a magical drink."

"It's your first day. I don't want to overtax you."

He was afraid to leave me back here alone, even as he took a step away from me, just in case.

"But if I don't learn, what about next time I work, or the time after that?" There was no way he wouldn't end up firing me.

A couple of people were examining the burned beard, smiling and nodding. Even burned-beard guy was nodding, as if this was somehow good.

"We'll figure something out," Zark said, looking out at the crowd as well.

This place was strange. Maybe this could last?

I'd just fallen asleep when the door swung open, slamming into the wall and jolting me awake. I scanned the entry for a herd of something bigger than grouslies heading over to eat me.

Instead, there was Zab, bouncing around. "I found you a place!"

"You did?" Even my sleep-deprived brain registered how fast he'd managed that. From what I'd known, he did like to entertain the ladies a lot. A homeless friend on your couch was definitely a deterrent to sexy times.

"Yes. Come on. I've got the keys." He was nearly vibrating, like he'd been plugged in.

"You've got the keys? They just gave them to you?" I shoved the hair out of my face.

"Of course. I already gave them payment. They have to. That's the way it works."

That cleared all the sleep cobwebs from my brain like a shop vac on a miniature dollhouse. I sprang up from the couch, grabbing clean clothes from the bag I was living out of.

"You told them I'd take it already? You paid for it?"

How much had I made yesterday? This place better be really cheap.

"That's how things work here."

"What do you mean?"

"Places don't open up for years sometimes. As soon as one is available, you take it."

"Oh, okay, then. Good work! How many coins do I owe you?" I asked, heading to the bathroom to get myself together.

"You'll never believe it!" he yelled after me.

It was small, but not more so than my Salem place had been. It had a wood stove in the center, which probably warmed the whole place nicely.

I was just about to tell Zab how much I loved the place when a dust bunny shot out from behind the stove and dashed across the room before disappearing. Then reappeared, dashed to another corner, and disappeared again.

Zab groaned beside me. "He should've told me there was a dust bunny."

"It's just a dust bunny. I'm sure I can get it to leave. The place is amazing, and I can't believe how cheap it is. You said five coin a month? That sounds ridiculous."

Zab was shaking his head and groaning again. "That's not a regular dust bunny. That's an Elusive Rare Dust Bunny. They used to only exist in Rest to torment people after they swept and vacuumed their house. Someone brought one back through a puddle, and they've become an invasive species. In Rest, they never show themselves, but here they don't stay invisible all the time. They don't have to with no known natural predators."

"Wait, they have predators in Rest?"

"Of course they do. Humans."

"But what about here?"

"Oh no, you can't chase out the Elusive Rare Dust Bunny. It was done once, and very bad things happened afterward to the chaser."

I had to live with a dust bunny? I looked about the place with a new eye. There was a thick coating of dust everywhere. I'd figured a good cleaning would take care of it, but what if it had just been cleaned? Oh no. This was bad. This was really bad.

"How long is the lease?"

"Uh, um..." He covered his mouth with his hand, shooting little glances my way before he'd look back over the place.

Oh yeah, I could totally believe the price now. It was all making sense.

"How long, Zab? What did you sign me up for?"

"Just, you know, the standard term. Nothing seemed crazy about it at the time. I thought you'd just lucked out."

And that was his first mistake. I didn't have good luck. Hadn't he figured that out yet? How long did you need to know me before that became apparent?

"What's the standard term?" I asked.

"Like...one hundred and twenty moon cycles?"

He took a step away from me. It was becoming a trend, it seemed.

"What... Wait, you don't mean... Is a moon cycle equal to a month?" What else could it be? Maybe a day? It was possible.

He shrugged.

"It's a month? I'm signed up for a decade with an Elusive Rare Dust Bunny?"

He inched toward the door. "You know, I've heard stories of people bribing them out. It could happen."

He was trying to help me. He was one of the best people I'd ever met. I needed to remember all these things before I killed him.

"Tippi? Are you okay? You know, you could always just stay with me. You don't have to move." He took a few more steps toward the door.

"It'll be... I mean, it's good. It's a good place. I'll figure something out with the dust bunny. I'm sure we can come to terms somehow."

It did another pass, as if marking its territory.

"Before I forget." He reached into his jacket pocket and extended his arm, holding out a book. "Housewarming gift."

"Thanks."

He shot to the door.

"Where are you going?"

"The dust is killing me. You can stay at my place, but I've got to get out of here. I think I'm allergic."

I waved him off. I couldn't live with him forever. I'd make it work, somehow.

The dust bunny shot past me again.

"Now you're just showing off," I yelled at it.

8

A bead of sweat dripped down my face as the stove kept blasting out heat, and my couch had turned out to be the only hugger in Xest. I must've missed hugs or something, because there was nothing about this in the magic book.

"I promise I'll come back and sit with you later, but you have to let me up."

Finally, the couch relented and I made it over to the stove.

"The room needs to be cooler," I said, flicking my hand toward the wood stove.

The fire went out completely. Not what I was hoping for, but I'd relight it after it was no longer a sauna in here.

At least the cocoa I'd set in the corner was gone and the dust bunny hadn't streaked a path across the place in hours.

I held up the new cocoa I'd just picked up. "Remember, if you want the cocoa to keep coming, you do your dusting *outside*."

A small chirping sound came from the vicinity of the

corner. I took that to be an agreement as I placed the cocoa down.

Now that the place was swept, I picked up Zab's housewarming gift.

The Handy Dandy Witch's Guide to a Happy Home by Matilda Marilda Hapilda

Furnishing Your New Home

There's nothing more unattractive than a home filled with new items. In this chapter, we'll take you step by step through how to create well-worn and previously loved furniture from scratch. With a few flicks of your wrist, a couple of words, you'll be on your way to a beautiful home, the envy of any witch and wizard, filled with items that look like they've been passed down through your family for generations. And remember, if something appears too new, you can always reabsorb the magic and start again. Don't settle for anything less.

I read the instructions. A couple of flicks of the wrist and a couple of chants and I'd hopefully have an apartment full of furniture. I scanned it all the way to the bottom, where there was the tiniest print possible.

Not guaranteed to work, especially for lower-level witches. Not guaranteed to last, especially for beginners. Spell only as good as the caster. Can't guarantee spells work for protectorates. We hold no responsibility if you use up all your magic on home décor.

.   .   .

Even in Xest, they covered their ass. Did people even sue here, or did they just turn you into a toad if they got mad?

Whatever. I needed a couch and didn't have that many coins yet. I'd take my chances, Matilda.

Mind focused, wrist flicking, chants flowing, I gestured toward the wall.

Whoa. I had a couch. It was a strange, tweed-looking fabric, a blend of greens, blues, and hot pink, but it was a couch and definitely worn. I took a few steps toward it and gave its cushion a press. Felt decent enough. I turned to sit, and a puff of dust shot up. Must have spooked the dust bunny.

There was a clucking noise.

"Fine. That one was my fault. I didn't mean to startle you with a couch. I won't take the cocoa back."

It appeared a few feet away from me and was staring at the couch, as if it wanted it gone.

"I need furniture. I'm a person."

Its ears went back and a little puff of dust went up.

"If we're going to be living together, I'm sure there are things you would like that I could do for you—like maybe a blanket and little bed of your own? That sounds nice, right?"

The bunny sat up on its hind legs, one ear going up as if it knew what I was saying.

"I could do these things for you, if maybe you could limit the amount of dust you put out just because I need furniture?"

Ear went down and then back, flat against its head. It disappeared. A second later, there was a huge dust cloud in front of me.

"We're going to have to come to a compromise."

More dust clouds. This place was going to look like the Dust Bowl again soon. Hopefully the bunny would calm down by the time my shift was over.

I grabbed my bag. "You just remember that they don't serve dust bunnies cocoa before you get out of hand."

It didn't respond, but it also didn't puff up any more dust.

I patted the dust off my jacket as I headed out. Zark's was across town from here, but the extra time in the fifth wind might be a good thing today.

The sun was setting, but it was still light enough to see the alternating nods and sneers as I made my way down the street. Eventually this would feel normal, as all things did, but it might take a tad longer than my typical adjustment period. I'd had no idea that I'd be such a polarizing person when I came back, not that it made me want to go jump in any puddles. I'd get used to the sneers, and they'd adjust to the fact that I wasn't leaving. But perhaps I'd stay to the main roads until a little more adjusting had been done.

I was so busy staring down the alleys I was avoiding that I ran right into a brick wall. Or Oscar, to put a name to him.

"Sorry. Didn't see you there."

"Yeah, I noticed you were preoccupied." He glanced down the alley himself, as if expecting to see a monster. "Something down there?"

"No. Just a shadow."

"Heading to work?" he asked as he fell into step with me.

"Yep. Thanks again for that. I owe you one." I owed him big. Without him, I wasn't sure anyone would've hired me, ever. Hawk had some serious pull in this place, even with the people who didn't like him.

"Not a problem." He was smiling a little too wide.

Was this a "stick it to your friend"-type deal? Was that why he was helping me stay? Didn't matter. Him sticking it to Hawk definitely helped me.

"Where were you heading?" I asked.

"Just happen to have some affairs that need to be handled down this way."

He didn't offer any more details, and I didn't press, not wanting to scare off my only jovial company. The amount of sneers heading my way this last leg of the journey was astounding. People didn't always cross the street for Oscar, but they didn't exactly get in his way, either, and I was enjoying the sneer buffer.

"Okay, well, I'll be off. Things to do and other debts to collect."

Zark's was only a few doors down as Oscar nodded and continued along. It might've been a coincidence, or had Oscar purposely walked me to work? I glance around, wondering if other people might've gotten the same impression. Would they all think I'd wanted protection? Well, I *had* liked it, but would they know? Or worse, would they think I sought it out? That wouldn't do at all. I'd leave fifteen minutes earlier tomorrow, just in case. I'd rather take a beating than look like I was afraid of them.

I walked into Zark's, and the place was busier than I'd ever seen. They all turned and looked at me nearly at the same time. At least here there was a room full of nods.

"Ah, Tippi, my dear!" Zark was waiting by the bar beside a young man with sandy-brown hair and big hazel eyes. I was pretty sure I recognized him from being out and about and not from getting sneered at. "This is

Gregor, my son. It's been so busy in here lately that I figured he could help you out when you work."

Gregor smiled. I tried to smile back even as the truth hit me. That was it. Gregor was proof. I was here for the crowds. I was a *fake* bartender.

"It's very nice to meet you." I nodded to the back room. "Uh, Zark, you think I could talk to you for a second?"

"Of course. Anything for you, Tippi." The rough and rugged personality of the Zark I'd first met had somehow transformed into the persona of a doting uncle who wanted to fulfill my every wish.

I smiled at Gregor again before walking away.

Zark spoke before I could get the chance. "Is there something wrong? Do you think you won't mesh with Gregor? I can get someone else to help you if that's the case. Your happiness is very important to me."

I was shaking my head before he finished. "No, not at all. Your son seems like a very nice man."

"Then what's wrong?" He stared at me like a man about to move the sun out of orbit if I said I didn't like the glare.

"Well, don't you think that maybe since I'm getting paid, I should do the bulk of the work? I don't feel like I'm doing much of anything."

Zark shook his head in painfully feigned shock. "You do a lot. Why would you say something like that?"

"I washed four glasses yesterday. That's it. That's all I did, all day." He might be willing to nix the sun and his son, but the line seemed to be drawn at messing with his bar.

He rubbed his jaw. "Are you unhappy about that? I want you to be happy here. Maybe you could wipe down the tabletops or something?"

If this job didn't work out, I was done. *And if you are listening, Helen, that does not mean I'm giving up. It just means maybe I might have to get very creative about my living situation.*

"Look, I like it here and I'm so grateful for the job. But if you're keeping me for the crowds, they're going to dwindle eventually after everyone gets their look. You know that. Then what happens? Will I get fired then when they're done eyeing me up and I'm not doing a good job? I'd rather be useful now and know I'll have a place to work."

There, it was all out on the table now.

Uncle Zark suddenly disappeared, and the craggy old man I'd first met was back. "Look, if you really insist on trying to do more, even though you're not good at it, we can work something out if it's going to keep you here. But as far as the crowds dwindling after they get their fill? It's not going to happen. That room out there? They think you've got something special that's wearing off on them. They're not leaving, and I'll pay you more if that's what it takes." He crossed his arms and looked like a man with a mission.

"I'm not looking for more money, but this is going to wear off." I hooked a thumb toward the packed room.

"I'm not so sure." He shook his head. "They think you're lucky, and I think they're right."

"You mean you believe it too? Trust me, I'm not lucky." I could give the man a long list to prove my point.

"Well, some might think you are. I've never made so much coin in one day."

"And when you figure out that I'm not?"

"I won't fire you because that won't happen."

There was a clear choice here: argue over why he

should fire the lousy employee, or be happy for employment. Did I really want to talk him into getting rid of me? I had an apartment and a dust bunny with a fondness for cocoa.

"Okay. That sounds fair. I'll head back to the bar now." Who was I to try to convince a man he was wrong? I was sure much better women than me had tried and failed.

"That's great. The crowd likes to see you. Try to stay front and center." He smiled, waving me off.

I made my way behind the bar, where Gregor was already filling orders.

"I'm really sorry you have to help me," I said. "I'm going to try to get better fast. It seems some of my magic gets a little excited at times."

His eyes lit as the corners of his mouth turned up. "It's fine. Rumor has it that you like to save up your magic for bigger things anyway."

"I didn't really plan that," I said, not wanting to start off a new relationship being a big magic showboater, especially when I couldn't even make a drink well.

"You'll find your way. I do have to say, a lot of us were surprised you came back. Word was you wanted out of Xest as soon as you got here."

He was wiping down the bar as he spoke, as if he didn't care that much and this was all small talk, but the gut I swore I was going to listen to said he was a little too interested.

"The place grew on me, I guess. It's hard to fit into Rest after the curtain is pulled back," I said, not imagining he'd understand. How could he when he'd never had to hide what he was?

"Any plans, you know, beyond this? I'd imagine someone as strong as you are would have some."

Ah, now all the questions made sense. Seemed everyone, from the sneers to the nods, was afraid I was going to rock the boat around here.

"I really don't. I'm just playing it by ear."

He let out a small laugh, as if elated to hear I wasn't determined to take over Xest single-handedly. Who did these people think I was? All I wanted was a nice little space to call my own, a job to pay the bills and maybe have half the population of Xest stop sneering at me.

9

Better shoes were in order for my new job. My heels were aching, and there were squishing noises coming from my feet. By the time I got to my place, it felt like I was walking in a slushie.

Nailed to the door was a long yellow scroll, nearly as tall as I was. Was I getting evicted already? What the hell was this? I ripped it off and brought it inside with me.

Letter from the Office of Immigration and Naturalization. You are hereby notified by the authority of all things magical in Xest that you need to present yourself first thing tomorrow morning regarding permanent residency in Xest.

The text became so tiny after that, I'd need a magnifying glass to read it. At the bottom was a raised seal.

Where was I supposed to present myself? Did I need a lawyer? Were there lawyers in Xest?

I rolled the thing up and headed back out.

I found Zab at the Watering Hole, his favorite bar, conveniently located within spitting distance of his place. He was at his favorite table with his friends, all of whom I'd met before.

He was having a drink. All the people at the table were familiar and greeted me with a smile. At least I was still welcome here.

"Zab said you were back. Sit! Have a drink!" Ab said, smiling like this might turn into date night suddenly. Berita was already pouring me a drink.

"I'd love to, but right now I need to steal Zab for a minute. Bit of an emergency."

Zab stood, looking guilty already. "It's the dust bunny, isn't it? What did it do?"

"No. I've got that under control. This is much worse."

"Worse than the dust bunny?" he said softly. Zab waved me outside. "I might not be back, so don't wait for me," he said to his friends.

"We should go upstairs," I said, motioning in the direction of his place. The letter would be a little conspicuous spread out on the sidewalk.

"What's happened?" he asked as soon as we got inside.

I pulled the yellow parchment out and unrolled it onto the floor. "This. I'm supposed to meet with them tomorrow morning. I've never heard of them before. Do you know what this is? Is it a trap?"

He took the scroll, which was hitting his feet. His eyes enlarged and he did a fast intake of breath. "Wow. I'd heard of them, but I've never heard of anyone actually going to see them."

"Why now? Why didn't they come for me before this? I was here for months before. I'm back for a couple of days and I get that?" I put my fingers to my temple, trying to keep a clear head over things and not think the worst.

He looked up, biting his lip. "I don't know, but maybe it's nothing. Maybe you had to be here a certain amount of time cumulatively?"

My guess was no. The list of people who wanted me gone was only half the population of Xest, would take a day to write down, and even then, I'd probably miss a few. There were people who hated me and I'd never seen their faces before. Zab was an optimist by nature. I could've plopped him down in the middle of an amusement park filled with princes and princesses and he'd feel right at home. I, on the other hand, mentally lived in the savanna, waiting to get eaten. I had a bad feeling that this situation was more tigers than royalty.

"Maybe I shouldn't go."

Zab gasped. "You have to go. You can't blow this off. You'll get kicked out of Xest."

"Shit. Shit. Shit." I walked around the room, wishing his place was bigger so I had more space to pace.

He tried to follow me but decided to take a central location and just turn with me. "Look, don't worry. I'll take the morning off and go with you. We'll figure this out. It'll be okay. You can meet me here in the morning, since the place we have to go is in this direction, according to the instructions."

I grabbed the paper back from the table he'd left it on. "What instructions? I didn't see anything."

"It's right there, see?" He pointed to some dots and dashes and circles. "These mean walk toward the sunrise in the morning."

"How will we know what building?" Were there more dots or wrinkles that were going to answer that too?

"Oh, that's easy. Government buildings only show up at appointment time. Whatever isn't there today will be it."

The obstacles to live here kept growing, but here was the only place I could ever be myself. How could I go back to Salem now? They'd have to let me stay. Somehow, I'd make this right.

"What if when I see them tomorrow, they kick me out?" I asked Zab. He didn't have an answer either, but there was no one else to ask.

"We'll figure something out."

My feet were sore and my head was pounding as I made my way home. I couldn't shake the eerie feeling that I was being watched, and after the note on my door, maybe I was.

There was a faint chattering in the distance, and I scanned the area for the source. Then I saw the Hear No Evil, See No Evil, and Speak No Evil monkeys running across the street toward me. They climbed up to my stoop, standing all six inches tall, in front of my door.

"What are you guys doing here? Does Marvin want to see me?" Even if he did, I wasn't going. I was too tired and too sick of Xest people right now, especially him and his factory. This night had already been too long several hours ago.

"We heard you bust people out of the factory?" Speak No Evil said.

"I don't bust people out. I helped one person relocate."

I wrapped my arms around myself. The walk from Zab's to my place hadn't been that bad, but the night had been that long. If I opened my door to go inside, would these little jerks follow me in? They *were* little. I could probably take all three of them at once if I had to. I could probably nudge them out of the way with my boot. It wasn't like they were that nice. Kind of obnoxious, if I remembered correctly.

I reached over them, opening my door to little cheers below me.

"I wasn't inviting you in," I said.

They didn't seem to care as they ran inside. By the time I shut my door, they were already on my couch. A trail of dusty prints led underneath where they sat. At least the dust bunny was accepting the furniture.

Ignoring my guests, hoping they'd leave, I moved to the wood stove.

"The air has the slightest chill and needs to be *warmed*." *Not hot. Please, not hot.* The thing burst into flames that looked like they'd been taken from the surface of the sun.

"You guys can't stay here," I said, throwing off my jacket.

"We have nowhere else to go," Speak No Evil said.

All three little faces looked at me. I knew what that felt like all too well. Still, I didn't like them. Did I really have to help them? No. They had to go.

But did they have to keep looking at me like that?

"Isn't Marvin looking for you?"

"He's mean. He makes us sit on his shelf all day. It's like a jail," Speak No Evil said, clearly the spokesperson for them.

I had to toughen up and couldn't afford to piss more people off by aiding and abetting Marvin's statues.

And then Hear No Evil started crying.

"Fine," I said. "You can stay, but just for tonight."

A little cheer went up, and then the three of them were doing flips on my couch.

"Only tonight," I said.

They stopped jumping to nod.

"Only tonight. Of course," Hear No Evil said.

They were never leaving.

I ran both hands through my hair and was heading toward the bathroom when Speak No Evil called after me, "I think you've got a dust bunny in here."

Two "ewws" followed.

I didn't answer as I shut myself in the bathroom.

10

Zab was waiting outside his apartment when I got there the next morning, looking down the street one way before looking the other direction. Nothing he saw seemed to make him happy. When he noticed me heading his way, I got a brief smile, but it slipped out of place quickly after.

"Why are you so nervous? Did you hear something?"

"I'll tell you on the way. We can't be late. Apparently they frown upon tardiness."

"But all they said was 'in the morning.'" Was this a Zest thing? Was *in the morning* an actual time?

"Doesn't matter. If your idea of morning is different than theirs, it's a problem."

He started walking briskly, as if his life depended on it as well as mine, because that was just who Zab was. He cared, maybe too much sometimes. If some girl ever broke his heart, I'd kill them.

Or maybe not. He did like the ladies a little too much, and not always the same one. My sweet Zab might end up being the heartbreaker, although certainly not on purpose. Either way, not a pressing problem at the moment.

If he walked any faster, we'd be jogging.

"Did you find something out?" There was a marked difference between last night's Zab and today, and I didn't think it was the couple of ales. He kept looking over his shoulder, like he expected someone to be following us.

"Yeah. I thought that they weren't around much because we so rarely have newcomers that stick around long. You know, because..." He gave me a look that said it all.

"They die too fast to bother."

He shrugged. "Something along those lines. Turns out this doesn't usually happen unless someone calls immigration in."

I hated when I was pessimistic and it turned out that I was right. Now to figure out who called immigration on me, which was going to be like climbing up a sand mountain.

"Someone hired Braid and Spike to get me here, and now someone else is calling in the government to get me kicked out. It makes sense, since I seem to be such a polarizing person these days. I could easily guess two names already: Raydam and Belinda. Maybe that weird little dude that said I was evil. He'd want to get rid of me for sure. What was his name?" Dammit. I had to remember for the list. It might be a sand mountain, but I'd be climbing it like I'd hiked my entire life. "Jasper! That was it."

"You're not blaming Hawk?" Zab asked.

"This might be the only thing I won't blame him for. Siccing Xest immigration on me wouldn't be his style. I'd be more inclined to believe he'd kill me himself first. Yeah, he's off the hook for this. Plenty of other people hate me, too many to count." But I was counting. I'd have to start putting names to the sneers. This would not go unanswered.

We were still walking to the edge of town when a building suddenly appeared at the end of the road. Zab was right. You definitely knew this one was different.

It was a single-story cottage that was bright blue and sparkled in the morning sun. The roof was covered in snow as if it had been here for a while, even though it hadn't. The windows glowed with light, but I couldn't make out any shapes or forms inside.

Zab waved me to run the last bit. "You have to hurry. You need to be standing in front of the door when it opens." He stopped short about five feet away while I continued until I was in front of the door.

"You can't come in with me?" I asked, looking back at him.

"Only if they invite me in."

I hated to continue to be the pessimist, but...

"If this goes badly, call Oscar. He might be able to help." He was the only one who might have enough clout to help me out if things went sideways, and also be willing.

"Got it."

The door swung open and a woman of undetermined but extremely old age stood in front of me looking like the quintessential witch, dressed in a black cape with stringy grey hair falling down her back. If the Wicked Witch of the West had looked like her, little kids would've run screaming from the theater. *I* wanted to run screaming.

She eyed me up thoroughly before glancing past me to Zab.

She pointed a bent finger at him.

"You are *not* invited." She turned around and walked inside. "Come in and shut the door."

One last glance back at Zab was all I got before I was shut into the room alone with her and two more witches. The other two were in the same black cloaks, same long grey hair, but one had ringlets. It did absolutely nothing to soften her look. The other was stirring a large cauldron over a massive fireplace. Dried plants and herbs hung from the ceiling as I walked across the wood-planked floor.

"She's the immigration call we received," the hag who'd answered the door said, seeming to have some sort of rank amongst the three of them.

"They said she was a Nowhere witch. Is that true? Are you a Nowhere witch?" the one with ringlets asked.

"No. Or, at least, I'd like it not to be. I still have magic and would greatly appreciate citizenship in Xest." I went to cross my arms but then kept them at my side, afraid of looking distant or defensive.

"We've already received a long list of why you shouldn't be allowed to stay," Lead Hag said.

I didn't care if it took a week. I was writing every name down until I found out who did this.

"Not to mention she's too short." This came from the shortest witch in the room, who was probably a good foot shorter than me.

"No. She's too tall, I say," the tallest one said.

Should I argue, or would that anger them? If I said nothing, that might not go well either. I tried to read the room, but nothing about this situation read well.

"She has no job," Lead Hag said.

"I do have a job," I said. That one wasn't an opinion. At least I could argue it.

Lead Hag got close enough that I would've sworn I smelled the grave she'd crawled out of. How old were these witches?

"Someone hired you? I thought you were a Nowhere witch. No one hires a Nowhere witch," Lead Hag said.

I'd never minded being called a Whimsy witch, though most would consider it an insult. But this "Nowhere witch" was like a rasp that kept running over the same piece of flesh, rubbing it raw.

"Someone did hire me. I'm working at Zark's." If I got out of here, I was going to have to thank Oscar several more times. I didn't care why he'd helped. I just knew I was on a razor's edge, and these witches were looking for any reason to get rid of me.

"She still has no home," Ringlet said, proving my point.

"I do. I just got it a day ago." Thank you, Zab! I was going to hug that dust bunny when I got out of here.

Every positive thing I had going for me seemed to build this feeling of anger in the room.

Suddenly, all sounds disappeared. The witches clustered together on the other side of the room, growing more animated. What didn't they want me to hear? Why was there an argument and why did not one of them appear to want me here?

I tried to stay calm as it continued, hating the loss of one of my senses, or that they'd taken it from me so easily.

They stopped arguing, and the sounds of the room, the boiling of whatever brew they churned, filled the space again.

The lead hag stepped forward. "You have one moon

cycle to return. When you come here again, you must bring fifty citizens of Xest to vouch for you. You must still be employed. You must have a residence. You must also pass our test of magic."

"Xest is a very desirable place to live. We can't just let anyone in," Ringlet said.

I wasn't sure which scared me more: the fifty people when I only had a handful of friends, or the magic test. Nope. It was the magic for sure.

"I'll be here." I infused my voice with a confidence that was all smoke and mirrors.

Even through the wrinkles, I could see the skepticism. Oh, someone had definitely given them an earful.

They stared. I pointed to the door.

"Yes. Go," Lead Hag said.

Zab stopped pacing when I opened the door. He waited until I got to him before he said softly, "How'd it go? Couldn't be too bad, since you're still here."

A swish of wind blew my hair forward as the building disappeared.

"Not as bad as I feared, but not great. I need fifty witches or warlocks to vouch for my character. I need to keep a job, a place to live..." That was all doable. It was the last bit.

"That's not so bad. I mean, fifty people isn't a drop in the bucket, but I think between just the people I know, it can be accomplished."

He was already mouthing names and counting in his head when I said, "Oh, yeah, I have to pass their magic test."

Zab swallowed, and there was no quick "it'll be okay" forthcoming this time, because we both knew it might not be.

Finally, with a shrug, he gave it his best try. "It's not like you don't have plenty of magic to work with."

"We both know it doesn't work the way it's supposed to. It does whatever it wants most of the time." I looked around, making sure the building hadn't popped back up. It was still gone, but I nodded toward the road, hoping he'd take the hint that we needed to be farther away before continuing our discussion. Those old hags looked crafty.

"My couch hugged me and wouldn't let go for an hour yesterday. I'm not sure how this test is going to go, but if it were for couches? That would be a fail. And forget heat. It was a sauna at my place. I nearly killed myself from heatstroke. The monkeys were even losing some of their glaze. Even when I do good things, it's because my magic decides it wants to. I have zero control over any of it."

"Then you practice. I'll help you. You can do this. You can because you have to. I might not be as strong as you are, but I'm very technical. I can teach you. I'm positive." He nodded as we walked.

"Hawk couldn't teach me."

"Hawk is more of an instinctive magic wielder. For this, I'm definitely better. You can do this. You can. This is going to happen." The more he talked, the more he tried to convince us both that it would work out, the worse I felt.

11

"There's no way he did that," the girl in the blue cap said.

"I'm telling you, it happened," the guy with flame-red hair replied.

"Old wives' tale, if you ask me. There's no way a Middling could get good enough at defense to fend off a Maker. No way in hell," Blue Cap said, shaking her head.

I'd been half listening to them for the past fifteen minutes, simply because they'd been sitting at the bar in close proximity. Now? I was a hundred percent invested.

I grabbed my rag and started polishing the taps that were a little bit closer to the duo.

"He did," Flame Red insisted.

"Then tell me how that's possible."

Flame Red glanced around, and I gave them my back as if I weren't listening to a thing they said.

In a softer tone, Flame Red continued, "He went up into Razor Hills and called on Bautere."

Blue Cap threw a hand up. "That's insane. They're more likely to kill you than help you."

"I'm not saying *I'd* do it, but that's the story. He went up there with an offering, and it taught him. If you have some serious magic coming after you, you do desperate things."

I knew they weren't talking about me, but it sure felt like that last sentence was directed right at me. Try having half of Xest coming for you. I didn't know who this witch or warlock was, but I understood completely.

Bautere. I'd have to remember that.

Gregor walked over and leaned by the area I was cleaning. "Hey, you want to grab a cocoa after work?"

Was he asking me out? Or was this a friendly outing? Dating right now was nearly out of the question with the amount of problems I had going on. It would be like taking someone on a stroll over quicksand just to have some company.

He was waiting for an answer with his smiling eyes. Poor sucker. He had no idea what he was asking for. He needed to be told.

"I don't know if it's a good idea to be seen with me socially. I've got some issues at the moment."

"Really? I hadn't noticed." He actually laughed, as if none of my mess bothered him. "Seriously, I'm not worried about those issues."

Gregor's eyes shifted over my shoulder. I was facing him, my back toward the door, and I still knew Hawk was here. This crowd tended to be quiet to begin with, never wanting anyone to hear what they were saying. When the soft murmurs died down even more, it could only be due to one person.

The patrons who'd been talking at the bar got up. I didn't want to turn around and deal with Hawk, but he was as stubborn as they came. He wouldn't leave until I did if I was his purpose.

"Do you want me to handle this?" Gregor offered.

"No. It's fine. He's here for me."

I turned, hating how my heart always did a little jump at the sight of Hawk. I was training myself to be a hardened junkyard dog, but somehow, deep in my chest, there was a golden retriever in there just jumping around, begging for attention.

I placed a coaster in front of Hawk, making sure he only saw the teeth and not the wagging tail.

"Can I get you a drink? There's a special on pitchers today. You get a free shred sandwich with each one."

I pretended to wait for his order when I, and everyone in that room, knew he wasn't here to eat or drink. He'd come to torture me. Get me fired. Kill me. Maybe all three, and in that order.

"We need to talk," he said.

That I hadn't expected. Didn't make me feel any warmer toward him. Well, except for the golden retriever that wanted to lick his face, but I was working hard on killing that damned dog.

"No, we don't."

Gregor stepped beside me. "Tippi, you don't need to—"

"I'm fine. Can you watch the bar for a minute?" Now I wanted to kill Hawk and Gregor. The only thing Gregor had accomplished was forcing me into a conversation with Hawk.

I'd felt Gregor's magic with an accidental brush of the hands the other day. He was no match for Hawk. I moved around him before he could continue trying to fight for me and got himself killed in the process.

I walked out of the bar, Hawk right behind me. If we were going to talk, this was not going to be a theatrical performance for the bar.

"Why are you here?"

"I need you to come to the broker house. I don't want to talk here." He took a step as if I'd just follow him. He still didn't get it.

"That's not going to happen," I said, not budging.

"I'm telling you, we need to talk," he said, staring at me as if I was short a few brain cells suddenly.

"This is it. This is all you get. A couple minutes in the street." I waved my hands around, indicating the spot where we stood.

His jaw shifted. Oh, that placid lake had white caps now. Good. See how he liked it when he was treated like the disposable help.

"You want to make it difficult, it's your call."

"I do. I like it difficult."

He was already walking off when I yelled, "The harder, the better." It didn't escape me that I sounded like I'd lost my marbles. The glances from the patrons about to enter Zark's confirmed it. Oh shit. I hoped they hadn't taken that to mean something of a more sexual nature.

It wasn't my fault. If they'd had to deal with him as much as I had, they'd be a little wobbly upstairs too. But they didn't. And why was that? Yeah, they all ran across the street when they saw him coming. The lot of them were big babies, and I would not be shamed by babies.

"We're in a fight, in case you all wanted to know," I told the looky-loos. "Because I'm not a scaredy-cat," I added, just so they'd know who they were dealing with.

Then I went inside before I looked even crazier.

12

My feet were sore, but I had a pocket full of coin. I might've made my entire month's rent in one night. It was as if every customer was trying to make amends for their initial slights and doubts with fat tips. Who knew what they'd been saying behind my back to feel this much guilt, but I didn't care if it was going to pay off this well. Maybe I could make them talk some more about me. If they'd seen me outside yelling, they'd have plenty of material.

Fifty coins, sixty, seventy, eighty...

Oof. My coins hit the ground as my head smacked into something hard. Except there was nothing there. I reached down and picked up my coins, took another step, and hit it again.

I reached out and felt something blocking my way that couldn't be seen. I backed up a couple of steps and rammed my shoulder into the area. Whatever was there, it was stronger than me. I tried moving west, and could only get a few steps. Same happened if I went north or south. The only direction I could head was east. I took a few steps, tried the other directions again, and found I could still only move east. I couldn't even turn around and go back in the direction of Zark's, where I'd just come from. A few more steps and the trend was obvious. The only way available was the way that led to the broker's office and *him*.

Oh, I'd go see him, all right. Each step had a little more force than the last, as the walk gave me time to stew over his high-handedness. What did he not understand about "stay out of my life"? That he wasn't entitled to my time? Did he think it was optional? He could leave me alone on his good days and screw with me when he felt the need for some entertainment? This was not how my life in Xest was going to be, and this time I'd make sure he got it through his thick head.

I slammed the door open, stepping inside the office. He was leaning against a desk, arms crossed, as if casually waiting for an appointment. In truth, I wasn't afraid of Hawk. If someone was going to commit violence tonight, it was me. He'd ship me off right quick, but I didn't think he'd physically hurt me. Trust was an altogether different beast, one with teeth that could bite if you put your hand a little too close.

"What the hell was that?" It was surprising there wasn't fire shooting out of my mouth as I spoke.

He raised his brows and shrugged, moving slightly as if to acquire a more comfortable position. "That's called a directional, or in common slang, all roads lead to Rome. Comes in handy when you aren't sure a newsflash will do the job."

Figured he'd get into semantics on the "what" and not the "why" of it.

"And I guess you're Caesar?"

"I told you we needed to talk." He smiled. I didn't believe for one second he was happy. As relaxed as he seemed, I could feel his edge like a razor pressed against my flesh. Yep, he was having a bad day, so he thought it was a good day to bother me. Wasn't going to happen.

"I told *you* I didn't care. Whatever you have to say, I'm not interested." If he'd acted like a normal human being and not corralled me into coming here, I might've heard him out eventually out of pure curiosity. Giving in to his domineering ways would only encourage future bad behavior, and that wasn't happening.

I turned toward the door.

"See, the thing of it is, you're going to have to hear me out." His voice was calm, like the lake that was hiding the Loch Ness Monster beneath its surface.

"And why is that?"

"I'm not lifting the directional until you do. If you were capable of protecting yourself at all, of resisting it, you wouldn't be here."

My lack of self-protection skills still seemed to get under his skin enough that he couldn't seem to pass up an opportunity to take a jab.

I didn't need any more hits after the last couple of days. I already felt like I was in the tenth round with Rocky. I'd marched over here, angrier than anyone else was capable of making me. Now I wanted to throw up the white flag. It was too much. *He* was too much. My feelings for him were a jumbled-up mess of what I'd thought we were, what I thought he was, and the truth. All I wanted was to go home.

"What do you want? Tell me so I can get the hell out of here."

There was a tiny little flicker in his eye. It was small,

and if I hadn't been staring so hard, I might've missed it. But I didn't. He had the nerve to be hurt after all he'd done to me? Even now, forcing me to come here and listen to him? I looked away. He might still be able to crawl under my skin now, but I'd hammer out any softness until there was nothing but hard, impregnable steel.

"I have a job for you," he said.

I let out a sigh as I rolled my eyes. The man was incapable of listening.

"I don't want it. If that's why I'm here then we can wrap this up right now."

"You don't have the option of turning this one down. You're the only one that can do it."

I shook my head. He wasn't winning this time. "I'm sure you can figure it out. After all, I'm not even supposed to be here, remember?"

I made my way to the door. I'd stand outside for hours if I had to. The door wouldn't open. Not a huge surprise, considering how Hawk did business. I looked around the room, trying to locate the best thing that might smash through the glass, focusing on the door, escaping, anything but him.

"There's a crack in the wall," he said.

I stopped scanning the room. There was only one wall I'd have any interest in, and it was the one I'd created. The one I'd nearly died making. The one that would protect this world from whatever evil thing that lived in the Unsettled Lands.

Now there was a crack, a weakness, a possible opening that could unleash hell. The visions of this place burning down, of Zab trapped, all ran through my mind again, as if *it* was here toying with me again. A shiver spread over my flesh and then settled somewhere deeper, in my chest, where it wouldn't leave.

I turned partially toward him, just enough that I could keep sight of him out of the corner of my eye but hopefully shield some of my horror from him.

"How bad?" Were we talking a hairline or a gap? There was a wide range of what could be considered cracks.

"They're slight, but they're growing. Figured as a future upstanding citizen of Xest, you might have an interest in keeping this place in one piece, especially considering how many enemies you've made simply by creating it."

There was only one word that caught my attention.

"*They*? How many cracks are there?" I turned fully toward him, wanting him to feel the depth of my rage.

Ideas, emotions all simultaneously clashed against each other. Of course I'd care. I'd cared before I'd been forced out. Had preached just this possibility, and look how that had turned out. If I'd been here, maybe I could've caught this earlier.

"Several."

Breathe. You need to breathe through the rage and get as many details as you could. "How long ago did they start?"

"About a month after you left."

A month and he didn't come and get me to try to repair it sooner. He had still tried to force me out of here, knowing, by his own admission, I might be the only one who could fix this. And he'd waited until now to tell me?

I swallowed back my fury. The more anger I felt, the more I raged against him, the more I'd let him in. That. Could. Not. Happen. Still, I couldn't drop it completely, either. He'd been wrong in an epic way, and there were no free rides in life, not even for the mighty Hawk.

"I distinctly remember bringing up this concern before I left. You said you could *handle it*. You said you didn't need me and that I should leave." The words hurt, even now. They'd burned so hot and deep that they'd left a scar that still stung at even the gentlest prod.

"But you're here," he said, looking straight at me, as if all that went before was water under the bridge. His water was a stream that led right to his monster waiting quietly.

"Yes. I am. But I don't work for you. I don't take orders from you. I don't *have* to do anything for you, not anymore. I don't need you." And I needed to get the hell out of here, away from him, and regroup.

"The wall is cracking. Are you saying you have no interest in doing something about it when you might be the only one who can?"

"What I'm saying is I'm leaving now. Lift your spell before I break it."

"So you figured out how to defend yourself finally?" he asked, straightening.

His eyes were steady on mine as he made his way across the room, toward me. Of course he'd call my bluff. It was Hawk. What else would he do but push the issue?

I stood my ground, hating the way his proximity sent a tingle of excitement through me like an addict about to get a fix. I used to think being near him was like sitting on the edge of a cliff, dangling your legs off. Now it seemed closer to dangling by my fingertips, knowing it all could be taken away in one second of weakness.

He'd given me a new life, a home, *while* he'd felt like it. When it had served his purpose. Then he'd ripped it away from me in a second. I'd never leave myself that vulnerable to him again.

He stopped right in front of me. His fingers grazed my

cheek, the tingle of his magic setting off waves of awareness that staggered my breathing. He dropped his head
down as his eyes seared a path to my soul, and other
places lower. Now what was his game? If he couldn't bully
me into it, he'd try to seduce me?

"You're wasting your time." My voice had a shadow of
the strength it did when I'd walked in here. I hated myself
for how much I didn't want him to stop at all. This was
why it was better to avoid him completely.

"You're so tough, make me. Show me your newfound
abilities," he challenged.

His hand, the only thing that touched me ever as our
bodies were only a hair apart, drifted until he threaded his
fingers into the hair at the base of my skull, tugging my
head back until our lips were aligned perfectly.

My body filled with longing, arching slightly as my
lips parted. But my pride wouldn't let me forget the one
and only time we'd kissed. How I'd melted into him with
no resistance, only to be turned away, once again. He'd
kicked me out of the home I'd made here and then kissed
me as if it was his right. Right before I'd been discarded.

I straightened and stepped back, losing ground but
regaining my dignity at the same time. His hand dropped
to his side. Once again, just like after he'd kissed me that
first time, he seemed annoyed, as if I were the one who
kept putting us in these situations. As if he hadn't been
the one to initiate the kiss that first time and now was
about to do so again. Yep, same old Hawk.

"I can't let this end this way, Tippi."

For the briefest moment, I thought he was talking
about us. Then I remembered why I was here. The wall.
The job he needed me for. Yeah, he liked me around as
long as he had a use for me.

If I could do something about the wall, I would. But I'd be flying solo this time. No boss needed.

I stepped away from him and walked to the door, hoping he wouldn't force my bluff about being able to get past his magic.

He didn't.

13

It was too late tonight, but first thing tomorrow, I'd go to the wall. I'd find every crack and fix them somehow, but I wouldn't be able to see anything tonight. The wall was way too big to try searching in the dark. Plus, I'd need all my energy, and right now I had nothing left in the tank.

I turned the corner, my place in view, to find the monkeys waiting on the stoop.

"We've got problems," Speak No Evil said.

"He's never said anything truer, and he's spoken a lot of truisms," Hear No Evil said.

"Yeah, we're screwed, from what I've seen so far," See No Evil said. "Landlord is here. Saw him coming and knew it was bad news just from the way he was walking up."

"He's inside?" I looked over their heads to my window above. This was the day that wouldn't end.

All three of them nodded.

"Do you know what he wants?"

"Don't know. Said he wouldn't talk to monkeys," Speak No Evil said.

"Or statues. He's got a thing against statues or something," Hear No Evil said.

"Jerk. We're going to see about him," See No Evil added. I hated to break it to them, but the humanitarian laws of Xest were pretty crappy for everyone. I'd barely escaped the broker's office not even an hour ago. If Hawk hadn't let me leave? I'd still be there, and there wasn't a soul in this place that would've been able to stop him. It seemed there was only one law that really counted in Xest, and that was "might is right."

I pushed open the door, knowing I'd have to get rid of the landlord before curling up under my blankets and going to sleep. The plan to make a bed tonight had been ruined a good hour ago. I could lie down on cement right now and fall asleep.

The dust bunny dashed across the room, making a run for the couch, as a middle-aged man chased it.

"I'm going to get you, you damn dust bunny," he yelled, shoving the couch to the side, the bunny moving with it.

He shoved the couch again, and the dust bunny disappeared from sight.

I'd never actually seen my landlord before. Zab had handled all the details. I wasn't impressed by what I was seeing.

"Can I help—" My voice was seized by a cough as the dust tickled my throat.

He turned, forgetting the dust bunny pursuit and giving me his full attention.

"You're Tippi?" he asked.

"Yes," I said, then cleared my throat one last time. "Why are you here? Zab said I was paid up until the first new moon?"

"You are, but you need to leave by tomorrow night."

"Why? Are people complaining about me? I've barely been here." Had the monkeys been annoying people while I was gone? I was going to kill those little suckers, who happened to be hiding behind the door with shocked little faces.

"No complaints. You just have to get out," he said, looking about the place as if sizing it up for the next tenant.

"Then why?"

"I have someone else who wants the place." He had the decency to look away.

There was only one reason I'd be getting the boot for no reason, just as I hadn't gotten a job.

"Let me guess. Hawk is behind this."

"Look, there's nothing I can do. He said you're out, so you're out." He turned his head, rubbing the back of his neck as his shoulders slumped. The aggression drained out of him like a big, fat helium balloon that had gotten popped.

"That's it? I get kicked to the curb because he says so?"

He turned, nearly pleading now. "You need to understand, I'm a low Middling man. I survive by staying out of everyone's way, and you're just too much trouble. You don't just have one side after you, but two now. I can't take the heat. It's not my fault you're a Nowhere witch and no one wants you."

The Nowhere witch. I'd thought Whimsy witch had been the bottom of the barrel, but the more I heard that name, the more I wanted to punch someone.

He pointed to the wood stove. "Leave the keys there on your way out." He looked at the couch as he was leaving.

"I've got an exterminator coming. You'll see who's boss tomorrow, dust bunny."

There was a squeak in the corner, like the thing had understood every word. What was an exterminator? I didn't think it would be the same type of profession I was familiar with in Salem, unless it was mob slang.

The door slammed shut and the monkeys rushed over.

"Well? What are we going to do?" Speak No Evil asked.

"We just got evicted. What do you think?" I asked.

"Oh no," Speak No Evil said.

"Really?" Hear No Evil asked.

I went and grabbed my bag of clothes, the ones I hadn't unpacked because I didn't have a bureau or trunk yet.

Speak No Evil called his two brothers over for a huddle. "We should've stuck it out over at the factory. Now we're homeless. Why'd we go with the Nowhere witch? No one wants her, and now we're outcasts with her."

"This was a big mistake. *Big*," See No Evil said.

"How was I supposed to know no one likes her?" Speak No Evil complained.

Hear No Evil was just listening on.

I'd lumped them all together before, but Speak No Evil was now my least favorite. Good. They could leave. I didn't need homeless speaking statues in my life. I had enough problems.

"Hey, you little jerks, I didn't invite you here. You crashed my place." I shoved a lime-green sweater in my bag.

The three of them looked taken aback at my comment.

"Why are you so sensitive? *We* like you," Speak No Evil said. "It was just a point of debate that a person no one likes might indicate problems."

I shook my head and continued gathering up the few things I'd accumulated.

The three monkeys walked back over.

"So where are we going?" Speak No Evil asked.

"It's *we* now?"

"We"—Speak No Evil motioned to the three of them —"took a vote. It's still we," he said, motioning me into the circle, while smiling as if he'd granted me a huge favor.

I shoved the rest of my things into a bag without answering. There was nowhere to go but the broker house or Zab's. I couldn't keep putting Zab out. He'd already put me up once and then found me this place, and if Hawk wanted me back at the broker house, which he clearly did, I wouldn't get another place.

Tossing the bag to the side, I sat on the couch. When that became too much to handle, I lay back and stared at the ceiling. The blank space was about all my brain could handle at the moment.

The monkeys were right. No one liked me. The only reason I cared was because I didn't know where to go. I was the Nowhere witch. No one wanted me.

I'd already put Zab out enough. Musso had a wife I'd never met, who probably wouldn't want a Nowhere witch either. Couldn't imagine anything but an awkward greeting there. It was too cold to sleep outside, and I'd never even seen a cardboard box in Xest anyway.

Hawk had left me no choice.

I closed my eyes, and the air filled with a screeching and banging blend that could make your ears bleed. I squinted one eye open to see the monkeys on a toy band kit that they must've found for the sole purpose of torturing me.

"What are you doing?" I asked.

"We're tense. We need to blow off some steam," Speak No Evil said, and then hit his little drum.

"Where'd you even find a band set to fit you guys?" I asked.

Speak No Evil shook his head. "We stole it off some kid. She was wasting it on some stupid dolls. Totally ridiculous. If she's going to treat her things that badly, then she deserved to cry." He went back to strumming his little guitar.

I choked as the dust bunny hopped onto the arm of the couch. Its little face came nose to nose with mine. Even the dust bunny felt bad for me.

Looked like I was going to be moving back to the broker building, but I wasn't doing it alone.

If Hawk thought he was going to force me to do things his way and there wouldn't be a price, he was dearly wrong.

I sat up, coming to terms with what needed to be done.

The monkeys were already perked up and waiting when I turned to them. Turned out, they had done me a favor.

"You got a plan?" Speak No Evil asked.

"She's definitely got a plan," See No Evil said.

"Pack it up. We're bringing everything, especially that stuff"—I pointed to their instruments— "to the broker house. We go tonight."

"We're moving to the broker house?" The three monkeys hopped up and down, holding hands and making a little circle.

A small squeak came from the dust bunny, who was sitting on the arm of the couch.

"Oh, you're coming too. Especially you."

We walked to the broker house like the vagabonds we were. I had all my possessions in a bag slung over my back. The monkeys followed in a row, all with their little luggage, except the bad musical equipment, which I'd offered to carry for them. Didn't want that to get damaged in the move. I wasn't sure I'd have the stomach to steal some kid's toy, and they'd be playing a lot if I had my way. The bunny hopped along, trailing behind us, leaving mud in its wake.

I pounded a fist on the door, and it swung open a second later. Why bother waiting for an invite when I'd be living here anyway? Hawk walked out of the back room, as if he'd been waiting. Of course he had. He'd gotten me kicked out and knew I'd be back shortly. He had also probably guessed I wouldn't wait until the morning to leave.

"I got kicked out, but you probably know that, don't you?" I stopped on one side of the room. He stopped on the other.

"I do what's needed. Right now, I need you working on the wall."

We eyed each other up like the adversaries we were. Or maybe that was my take on it. In his mind, I was still an employee. If he thought that was the way this was going to work, that I'd sit here and willingly take orders, he was drinking fairy juice.

"I guess I can't work on the wall unless I'm here?" I raised a brow.

"You've made quite a few enemies. I can't let them kill you before it's done." He said it with a shrug, as if he was funny.

"I won't be working on *anything* for you." He could kick me out right now, too. I'd sleep in the alley before I'd let him boss me around.

"Consider it free rent while you think things over." He moved to the side, stepping out of the direct line of sight to the door that would lead to my old bedroom.

"I'm not considering anything. I have nowhere else to live."

He walked over slowly, because Hawk never rushed anywhere. He stopped a couple of feet away, his hands in his pockets, relaxing.

"Then just consider it free rent," he said.

At least I was killing his humor. He looked to be stewing in a pot of venom, right alongside me. That was something.

"I'll need an extra room for my companions," I said, trying to sound like I was all steely resolve instead of wondering if I should've fought with the landlord or tried to find somewhere else.

His gaze went to the three monkeys standing beside me. The dust bunny hopped closer until it was sitting on my other side, and then became invisible as I felt it press against my leg.

Maybe I should've gone to Zab's, but it wasn't just me anymore. The monkeys had debatable worth and likability at times, but they didn't deserve the factory, no matter how annoying they might be. For some reason they'd chosen to be with me, and I'd let them. How could I kick them to the curb now? Then there was the dust bunny. No one wanted a dust bunny. No. One. But to leave it to the exterminator? Nope. It was what it was. They were mine to care for now, and since Hawk had stolen our newly found home, this was it.

"Fine."

He had no idea what he'd just agreed to.

I wouldn't thank him. The only reason we were here was *because* of him. They wouldn't need anything if he'd left us alone.

He'd thought he'd won, but the game had just begun.

14

I woke up in the same bedroom I'd begged to keep, except that this was the last place I wanted to be at the moment, even as part of me had missed the place. Now it only reminded me of what had gone down and how I'd been forced out.

There was a Do Not Disturb sign hanging on the door next to mine. The monkeys and the dust bunny had made themselves comfortable.

I didn't have to be at work for a few hours, so I might as well make myself at home and go say hello to the guys. That was at least something I looked forward to. And if Hawk was there? I would not be talking to him.

Same bed, same bathroom, same walk downstairs. I'd wanted to be back here so badly, and now look at me. Every step was irritating me. And yet not. There was a comfort when I ran my hand over the wall near the third step and felt the subtle bump. The second step creaked the loudest, and the first sounded a little like a cat's meow. When I opened the door to the office, I'd see Zab, who'd greet me with a smile. Musso would give me a grunt and a nod that was somehow just as welcoming. Helen's gears would kick up a hair when I entered the room, as if she were happy to see me too. It all felt too familiar, too much like home. I hated that Hawk had given this to me and then taken it away.

Still, there was a slight hitch in my breathing as I opened the door. I wasn't just back in Xest. I was *back*. It felt so right, and it was all so wrong. This wasn't the way it was supposed to be.

Still, I swung open the door, and it creaked at the last moment like I knew it would. I stepped into the office and got the smile from Zab, got the grunt from Musso, got the churning of gears from Helen.

I also got a lavender head of hair on the cutest face I'd ever seen, sitting at *my* table. What was she doing at *my* table? She looked up and had the nerve to smile. I was glaring the way Belinda had at me.

It was all so right and so wrong.

Her face fell and Zab stepped into the gap, the way he always did. "This is Bibbi. She's new. Bibbi, this is Tippi."

Bibbi smiled again, this one more hesitant. I got a hold of myself and reeled back on the Belinda that had just taken over my body.

"Hi, Bibbi. Nice to meet you." I forced my upper lip into something that might resemble a smile as I scanned my table. She was using *my* baskets. She had *my* flower. That was *my* stuff. I'd taken it from other parts of the office fair and square. Why did she have *my* stuff? Couldn't she go get her own?

"I liked your décor, so I left it. Hope you don't mind."

Her smile was still there, but her eyes kept slipping over to Zab, as if she were looking for reassurance I wasn't going to kill her and then eat her.

Zab gave a subtle nod and patted the air, as if to reassure her. I tried to smile again. She took a step back.

"Let's go get a cocoa," Zab said, going to the coin box.

"Sure." Just like old times, and yet not. This might've been the worst case of déjà vu ever.

He nodded at Bibbi one last time before we left. She waited until we were out the door before she sat back down at *my* table.

"I wasn't trying to scare her. It was a lapse. You could've warned me." I mean, I hadn't been that scary, had I? Yes, I'd had some bloody thoughts, but they'd just been thoughts.

Zab wasn't paying any attention to what I was saying as the street seemed to part for us.

"Is this what it's always like now?" he asked, watching the sneering and nodding from the people passing by.

"Yeah. I barely notice it. So who is she?" I asked, dragging his attention back to the problem.

"Just someone Hawk hired her after you left."

"To do what? Why is she in my spot? Why isn't she at Belinda's desk?" Belinda's desk was much nicer. She could have it. She *couldn't* have my table.

He cleared his throat. "Because he hasn't replaced Belinda yet."

I stopped walking. Zab walked another couple of steps before he stopped as well. When he turned, his face was scrunched up tighter than a tinfoil ball, his eyes squeezed shut, as if he were scared my expression alone might scorch the ground he stood on.

"He didn't replace Belinda, whose job was more important, but he went out of his way to replace mine, a job that hadn't existed before?" There was only one thing that said. Hawk had wanted to wipe my memory clean from the place. Bibbi was his palate cleanser after a bad meal. He couldn't wait to get rid of me because apparently I'd left a horrible aftertaste. And now he was forcing my hand so I had nowhere else to stay but there? Why?

Zab opened one eye a sliver. "It turned out that your position was very useful."

"Did you ask for someone because I'd made your job easier?" A glimmer of hope sprang to life in the midst of a pile of crap. If Zab had asked, it would've been because he missed me and was trying to find a replacement for his good buddy. Seriously, he needed someone to go get cocoa and chat with. Musso wasn't a big talker, after all.

"Not really," Zab said.

My glimmer had a sledgehammer hanging over it. "It's a yes or no. You either asked or you didn't."

"Then no."

Back to the foul aftertaste for me. "How fast did he hire her?"

He looked away.

"Zab, how fast?" I asked, crowding him.

"I don't know. Time is different here than in Rest. I think a week there is actually seven days here."

"A week *is* seven days. It's the same. Now how fast did he replace me? Just spit it out."

His shoulders went up, and it looked as if he would've tried to bury his head in them if he could. "I mean, maybe a day or two after you were gone, give or take a couple of hours?" He put his fingers to his temple, poised suspiciously close to his ears.

He didn't have to worry. I wasn't going to yell. I was beyond yelling. I had the quiet, boring kind of anger.

"Same day, huh? Didn't even get a good night's sleep, did he?"

"I know it looks bad, but—"

"I don't want to hear about how he wasn't the same after I left, because he didn't skip a beat."

I really was the Nowhere witch and Hawk was keeping me here because he needed me alive. That was the beginning and end of it all.

"It doesn't matter anyway. I have bigger issues." The immigration list, the wall breaking, and that was only the beginning of it. Forget someone taking over my table. I might not even be allowed in Xest at all soon.

"As to that, can you come by my place tonight? The sooner we get started, the better."

"I'll be there with cocoa in hand." The less time I spent at the broker building, and around Hawk, the better.

15

As promised, I had a cocoa for each of us as I walked into Zab's place.

"Good, you're here," he said. "We've got a lot to do in a small amount of time."

"What's that?" In the center of his apartment, on the top of his wood stove, was a black pot that looked like it might've come out of some fairytale, and then been reused for another fifty fairytales before someone left it out in the rain to rust over.

"It's a cauldron for brewing potions. It's part of your curriculum I've been working out. We need to cover all the bases with what those old crones might ask." He grabbed a book lying on the table, flipped it open, and slid it over to me.

One quarter cycle each:
 Cauldron and potions
 Amulets and tokens
 Wards

Review and practice for final week leading up to appointment.

"They might test you on defense and offense. Since that's not my strength, we might have to ask..."

I jerked my gaze to his, daring him to say Hawk's name.

"...Oscar or someone else," he finished, smartly changing his answer. "I'd do it, but I'm not good enough in combat to teach anyone. What you've done already on instinct way surpasses my abilities."

He was right. I needed to be prepared in that area as best I could. Problem was, if I asked Oscar, he might tell Hawk. I'd already been down that road and hadn't liked the terrain even on much sunnier days in our relationship.

But there was another very solid option.

"I think I can handle that on my own," I said.

"You sure?"

"Yeah. I've got something in mind." I turned to the cauldron, trying to do a fast bait-and-switch with the conversation before he delved any further into plans he wouldn't want to hear or agree with.

He took a rag and wiped out the cobwebs inside.

"Do people use these things much?"

"It's a rarer field of practice. A lot of the old-timers like them, though, and they have their purposes." He blew into it, trying to rid the thing of the last bits of dust and debris.

I backed up as some rust flakes headed for me.

"Why not just do a regular spell?" I wiped some gunk off my eyelashes.

"Spells are more of a broad magic. This is the stuff you

go to when you need finesse and precision. Don't mind its size. I never splurged on a bigger one. This is a hand-me-down, but it gets the job done."

"It looks like a very nice cauldron. So what are we making?"

He put the cauldron on the wood stove, smiling at his achievement. I was just hoping we didn't have to eat anything out of that thing.

"Do you cook stuff to eat in that?" I asked, figuring out an excuse for lunch if needed. I might be on a cocoa-only diet starting today.

"Definitely not." There was a pause and a shrug before he added, "Well, *mostly* not. I might've used it for soup on the odd occasion, but that's not what it's meant for. Let's say you want a guy to notice you but you don't see him much. When you do, it's in a crowded situation, and maybe you don't want people to know what you're up to. That's when you drag out the cauldron."

He grabbed another book by the couch, brought it over, and flipped to one of the many dog-eared pages.

"I was going through this last night. There are basics that they might look for, but none of them will be easy to test. The love potion. The illness. The cure. The hate. Still, it's better if you know them to be safe. There's also another potion—it's harder, but I've got a gut feeling they might throw something like this at you just to take advantage."

"What is it?" I asked, trying to look at the page he'd marked.

"A time-reverse potion. It's basically like the fountain of youth. It's not easy, but I think we add it in anyway."

"How much harder is it?"

"You'd need to be at minimum a high Middling and also have infinite magic, because it's a real depleter."

"Can I do that?"

"You're kidding, right?" He pushed the book toward me.

"Not really. I know I've done some interesting things, but maybe I'm using up everything I have. What if I'm going to run out soon?"

"You and Hawk never talked about this?" Zab grabbed a nearby stool and sat.

I took the seat opposite him. "No."

"That's crazy. One of the most important discussions people have, and from a young age, is how much magic they have. It determines so much of their future. Didn't you ask? How did you not want to know?"

"When I first got here, I was set on getting out. Then, for a while there, I wasn't sure it was such a good idea to know, because it seemed to increase the attention I was getting. By the time I was back in Salem, other than Rabbit, there was no one to ask. And even if she could shed some light on it, I wasn't asking her. She'd just lost everything because she'd run out of magic. How could I bring it up with her?"

"Well, now that we're talking about it, if you weren't infinite, that wall you built would've wiped you out. That was an epic amount of magic to lay out. Even for a Maker, I wouldn't have been surprised if you'd slept for a week after that one. The fact that you got out of bed the next day means you replenish fast. I don't know enough about the upper magic workings, but I'd say you got dealt a good hand. If those hags want to get you out, they might go for something like this first, trying to weaken you."

"Okay, so what do we do?"

He pointed to a trunk in the corner "We aren't doing anything. You are going to go through that basket of supplies while following the instructions."

I brought the book over to the trunk he'd pointed to and opened it up. There were all sorts of bottles and flasks, filled with powder, liquids, and goopy things. They all had faded labels that looked a hundred years old.

"Is this stuff still good?" I tried sneaking a discreet sniff of the contents.

"Yeah. The trunk was spelled to preserve it." Zab's breezy answer wasn't a real trust builder.

I went through the list, finding the corresponding items, trying to not think of the names. Sometimes, though, when I was looking for frog guts, pigeon eyes, and tongue of a long-deceased liar, it was a bit tough to pretend this wasn't what it was. It all came down to one thing: how bad did I want to stay in Xest? I'd gag, pause, and continue.

I assembled all of the items in the cauldron warming on the stove. "Now what?"

"Just stir. Whoever stirs the pot infuses their magic into the potion. That spoon acts as a conductor."

Fifteen minutes later, we were bubbling up to a nice boil. The stuff smelled horrible, but my magic, for once, didn't act up. Or I hadn't thought it did. The stuff I'd made smelled like a rotting corpse.

"I'm not sure about this. It smells like an aging potion," I said to Zab, who was flipping through some more potion books on the couch, dog-earing quite a few.

He got up and poked his head over the cauldron. "No, that's right. I've smelled this before."

"How are we going to test it? I don't want to be any younger."

He stared at the cauldron. "Neither do I. I'm not sure. Maybe we could give Musso some? He could handle getting a couple years knocked off."

If he wasn't offended by the offer, that would lead to other issues. "He'll tell Hawk."

"He might not have said anything, but I'm sure Hawk has heard about this already. He hears everything."

There was a difference between Hawk hearing and reminding him. He hadn't said anything yet, and I was going to try to keep it that way.

"I don't want to tempt Hawk to get involved, and I feel like bringing this to the office in any way would." In Salem, there would be a line out the door for a place offering youth. How much different could it be here? Certain things had to be universal.

"How many years will this take off someone and for how long?" I asked.

"Depends on the witch or wizard who made it. With your magic, it might take off decades. I'm not sure how long it'll last. Once in a while it's permanent, but that's really rare. I'm not sure how strong you are, so it's hard to say. Plus, they aren't done a lot because they use up a lot of magic. That's why there aren't only twenty-year-olds in Xest. They'd deplete all their magic trying to stay young and then die early. You'd need to be an Infinite to keep it going." He leaned over the cauldron again, taking a deep whiff. "Sure smells strong, though."

I kept stirring, not sure if this stuff could burn. "So the stingier someone is with their magic, the less they have?"

He walked over to the trunk while he answered, "Sometimes. Other times they're stingy because they don't want people to know how much they have. It's also considered bad form to throw magic about a lot. It's like bragging." He was rifling around in the bottles. "Ah. Here we go. You can use this to bottle it up until you find a tester."

I glanced back at his trunk of old stuff. "Hey, do you happen to have a map of Xest in there? Or some book on the lay of the land? Just in case they ask me questions about the geography?"

"Sure." He went to a shelf in the corner and handed me a rolled parchment. "You can keep it. I don't need it."

"Thanks."

"You ready to call it quits for the night? You're probably pretty tired after that." He took another look at me. "Aren't you?"

I wasn't tired at all, but I did have some other things to handle. I faked a yawn.

"Definitely ready for bed."

Two sweaters layered under a thick jacket and it was still freezing up here. But this was where I needed to be. There was one thing Hawk had been right about from the beginning, even if I hadn't wanted to hear it. If I couldn't figure out how to protect myself, I'd be a sitting duck, waiting to be plucked up or shot, targeted by anyone who wanted to use me or get me out of the way.

The map said Razor Hills was right past this bend. Hopefully my offering would be enough to keep Bautere from killing me before I had a chance to talk to it.

I crept along, trying to be as quiet as I could until I was close enough to call for it, holding out the offering. And if it didn't want to be young again, or if it was already immortal, at least I'd be running downhill.

I hadn't walked more than a few more paces when I could feel eyes on me. I slowly took the bottle out of my pocket, in case it was assessing me for a threat, and held it in the air as I turned.

"I've brought you an offering," I said loudly, hoping I wasn't yelling at squirrels and chipmunks.

There was a low growling noise as some branches and twigs snapped. The gossipers at the bar hadn't explained what a Bautere *was* when they were gossiping at the bar. Was it too late to run? Maybe not. Was I going to run? The old Tippi would've. That probably meant I should stand my ground.

It went silent again, and I had a feeling that had been my first test. Or my only warning before I was a late dinner.

I didn't hear it approach. I hadn't known it was so close until I made another full turn and it was there and I jumped back.

It was fifteen feet tall, standing on its hind legs, a strange cross of a polar bear and a man, with humanlike eyes and a blended body of both.

It growled low and deep as I clenched the bottle tighter, afraid it would slip in my sweat-slicked grasp.

"This is for you." I knelt, reaching out as close as I dared to place the bottle in the snow.

He walked confidently toward it while I took a few steps back. He uncorked the lid and sniffed.

"A time-reverse potion," he said, the words flowing through a muzzle that should've been made for growling and tearing flesh from bones. He sniffed it again. "It's potent." He lifted his muzzle in my direction, taking a deep breath. "It has your magical scent on it."

I nodded.

He corked the flask again and then eyed me from my shoes to the tip of my hat. "What do you want?" he growled.

"I need to learn how to fight." This definitely wasn't a want, with the number of enemies I had and now the three hags on my tail. My life wants had been whittled down to necessity only. If it was something that could wait, it did.

His lip curled back. "I know who you are. You have others who can teach you. There are other options for you that might suit your human fragility better."

I shook my head. "That's the thing. I don't want to be fragile. I can't afford to be."

If I wanted to survive, there was no room for softness, no matter the cost.

He dropped down onto all four paws, still a good six or seven feet tall, and circled me.

I stood still, letting him take my measure.

He walked back and stopped in front of me.

"No arguments, you do what I say."

"Yes."

"Then so be it."

He growled and swung a paw in my direction. I slammed into the ground, and I knew Bautere had pulled his swing.

"Get up," he said.

"We're starting now?" I asked, wiping the snow from me.

"You think you get to choose when you fight? Yes. Now."

16

The monkeys had decided they needed an audience and had set up on top of a bookshelf in the office. The missed chords and off drumbeats echoed through the door before I even walked into the office that morning.

Oh, this wasn't going to be good.

I strolled in as if nothing were amiss, as if I didn't feel like I'd been turned inside out by Bautere, like the monkeys weren't torturing people with their music, and like I didn't see dust bunny tracks trailed across the floor.

"Hey, all," I said with a smile, as if everything was good. I might've added a little too much perk to sound natural and had declared my guilt instead.

Musso's grunt was a little rougher than normal. Bibbi wasn't looking up from *her* table, too scared to make eye contact.

Zab looked up at me. "Haven't I always been a good friend to you?"

"They're not *that* bad." I glanced over my shoulder at the monkeys before turning back to him. "They're actually improving a little."

"Everybody's a critic," Hear No Evil said from his perch. The rest of the band was shooting Zab dirty looks.

Of course the dust bunny decided to streak across the office right then.

"Dusty, I told you, outside only," I yelled in the direction I thought it went, guessing by the plumes.

"You named it?" Zab asked right before he coughed. He went to take a sip of his cocoa but put the cup down. "It stole my cocoa again."

Ah, shit. I'd forgotten to get it cocoa this morning. Although Zab was the last person who should be complaining about the bunny. I'd take the heat for the monkeys, but that was where I drew the line.

"Hey, the dust bunny problem is as much your fault as mine," I said.

He groaned softly as he slumped, covering his face. Musso was shaking his head and Bibbi was still looking straight down, afraid to glance up at me.

"Look, I'll get you another cocoa as soon as I get back from my errands," I said, grabbing my coat before the band started back up.

The last thing I would do was hang around the office and wait for Hawk to show up while I watched Bibbi do my job. I hit the street, ignoring the sneers and nodding back when it was appropriate until I made it out of town.

I hiked my way up to the wall, spending my time wondering if Helen wrote Bibbi notes and ground her wheels a little faster when *she* walked in. It fueled me up the hill a little faster, and without one of Hawk's nifty doors, it was a long haul. Even with two layers of socks and the heaviest clothes I owned, the fifth wind seemed to favor the mountain.

Hopefully Hawk would be off handling something

else, somewhere else, and he wouldn't get the satisfaction of knowing I was up here, that I cared about the cracks in the wall, though of course I did. This place was my home too. It had been before he'd booted me, and I didn't need anyone to tell me to protect it. Seriously, *I* was the protectorate. Who did he think he was? Offense didn't tell defense how to guard the goal. He needed to stay in his own lane and stop acting like the king of everything.

The second I got up there, I remembered why I'd hated this place. It felt worse than when I'd left it. That feeling, the soul-sucking dread that made you think you'd rather be dead than live another minute, was seeping back into the area. You could be having a perfectly splendid day and the second you felt it, it was as if the world around you was burning down and screaming in agony. It wasn't full force, but it was growing again.

Right after I'd done the spell that built the wall, it had gone away. Or I'd thought it had. Maybe I'd been too out of it to notice by that point. It was here now, though, its dark magic leaking out and getting its tendrils past my barricade.

Not only was the evil feeling back, but the hatred too. This thing hated me with a special kind of intensity, and I didn't think it was just about the wall, as insane as that might seem.

Either way, something had to be done. There was no doubt that there were breaks, but could I repair them? I hadn't really known what I was doing the first time. What if I messed the wall up and made the weaknesses worse?

I was getting ahead of myself, though. First I had to find them. Easiest way to do that was to follow the feeling of dread. I took a step to the left and wallowed in the misery for a minute before taking a step to the right. Oh yeah, definitely to the right.

"I could've gotten you here faster," Hawk said.

"Are you following me?" The cold melted away as my blood boiled. I shot him a look over my shoulder that told him how I felt about company.

"Of course not. You hiked up here. Why would I possibly do that?"

"You just happened to be here when I came?"

"You seem to forget that this has been my concern before you even knew Xest existed. You said you weren't interested in the cracks, so why would I think you'd be here?"

That was a valid point, not that I'd tell him.

I took a few more steps, following the feeling of dread and ignoring the hitch in my heartbeat that seemed to come whenever I saw Hawk. Why had I imagined that it would be gone after not seeing him for a few months? Or after he'd booted me out like last night's trash? Clearly, I wasn't sane enough to feel what I should. Luckily, I was sane enough to do what was right: stay away from him as much as possible.

"I'll show you the spot," he said, walking with me.

"I can find it on my own. You should just go about your business."

This wasn't going to be a little outing, where we pretended things were like old times. There would be no working together in any capacity. He'd shut the door on that months ago.

"I didn't come here for you. I came here to check the wall, the way I do every day," he said, still walking the same way I was heading.

I stopped. He continued in the direction I wanted to

go. "Then go check out the rest of the wall. You don't need to come this way right now. There's plenty more to do."

"You go to the other side of the wall if you want to be alone." He kept walking.

"I'm not changing my direction." I kept walking.

"Why do you seem madder than you were last night, after I got you evicted? Is there something new you're angry about?"

He might as well have asked if I wanted a second piece of toast, as concerned as he sounded. Although how he'd noticed was beyond me. Maybe he had some rage-meter spell on me.

"I don't need anything new. You've done plenty already." I wasn't that much angrier after seeing Bibbi and finding he'd hired her the same day he tossed me out. I'd been nearly this angry all along. That was just the latest insult.

I trudged along in the snow, trying to walk fast enough to put some distance between us but still get a good look at the wall as I went.

The first crack appeared and stole my breath away. It was small, but the way it feathered out was alarming. It reminded me of one of those dings you got on a windshield that slowly kept growing until it took up the entire thing. I ran a finger along it, wondering if my spell hadn't been strong enough for the evil it was trying to contain or if something else was trying to help it out.

I put my entire palm on it, trying to fuse it back but not really having any idea how I'd made it in the first place. I put my other palm on it, trying to imagine the crack healing, trying to force the magic inside of me outward to the wall.

"Do you remember anything from when you made the first one?" Hawk asked.

"Pain, misery, and then instinct. An instinct that seems to be selective," I said, the wall suddenly washing away my concern over whether or not I talked to Hawk right now.

I backed up, looking at the spot for some sort of change. Had I accomplished anything? Maybe it was a hair shorter, or was that in my head?

"Does it look any different?" I asked him.

"Same," he said.

"Are you sure? Maybe it's a tiny bit smaller?" I backed up a little more.

He pointed to a nearby tree. "See that? I mark the trunk every day. It's grown at the same pace it did yesterday, and the day before."

I walked farther, looking for more. He kept walking in the direction of the next one. It was almost idiotic not to follow him, not that I didn't consider it anyway. The cracks were more worrisome than his presence right now, though.

"Show me the others," I said, dropping any pretense of not caring about the wall or keeping my distance. That ship had sailed as soon as he'd seen me here, and at least he wanted this wall fixed as much as I did. If I could use him for help here and there, I'd be stupid not to.

He headed uphill, following along the line of the wall, the snow getting deeper as we went. It was nearly knee-high in a couple of hundred feet.

I swayed to my left, nearly falling with the height.

Hawk reached back, grabbing my arm and righting me. I pulled back the second I got my balance back. I wanted to yell at him that I didn't need help but held my tongue. If I'd fallen and he'd let me land on my ass, I would've been burning up over that too. The truth was that, at this point, Hawk could do no right. He'd done too many wrongs.

I couldn't focus on him, though. I couldn't add anger to the already bad mix of emotions I got around this place. The feeling of dread that had begun to fade was on the rise again. The next fracture was near.

He stopped in front of the next crack, the sun hitting it clearly and showing that this one was definitely worse. If you ran a hand across the spot, there was a distinct unevenness.

"How many more?" The dread in my voice had nothing to do with the feeling it gave off. Until this was fixed, this worry was going to cling to me no matter how far I got from *it*.

"There are five in total at the moment. There was a new one every week for the first few weeks. This week there were two new ones."

"Five and they're accelerating." I stepped back so I could see my creation more clearly. I shivered and didn't know if it was the cold or the reality stinging me. Even though I'd made this crazy wall of crystal, or whatever it was, I had no idea how—or how to repair it.

Hawk shrugged out of his coat beside me.

"I don't need your jacket." I took another step away from him before he could try to put it on my shoulders.

"You're shivering," he said, his arm outstretched still.

"I'm fine. I don't need your help, and I don't want you to think we're going to work together like we used to." I wouldn't look at him even as his eyes bored into me. He'd always had more patience than me, but that seemed to be flipping. It was nice to play the calm one for a change, even if it was only in comparison.

He stepped closer. "If you don't take this jacket, I'm going to tie it on you."

I looked at him now, my eyes narrowing. "You would, too, wouldn't you?"

"Yes, I guess I would. I'm just a real bastard like that, not wanting you to freeze to death."

"Don't try to pretend you're a good guy. You played that game before, and it didn't hold up well in the light of day."

"I've been accused of a lot, but I don't think I've ever heard that one before. If you thought I tried to play a good guy, you weren't paying attention."

He was right. There was nothing good about him, even then. He'd been protecting an asset.

He still had his coat held out to me, and there was a promise in his eyes. I took it, but only because I'd lose the fight. I wouldn't always, though. I'd guarantee that.

He moved. I followed him because I needed to see how bad the rest of the cracks were, whether he was there or not.

We surveyed the final three weak points in silence. When we were done, we lapped back to the door he must've used to get here.

He walked over to it, holding the door open as he stared my way.

"I was going to take it anyway," I said, walking past him and into the hallway of the broker's office.

I made my way downstairs, and not because I was looking for company. I needed a hot tea or a second-rate cocoa, or anything that could put some warmth back into my body. He followed me downstairs, perhaps under the misunderstanding that we'd be speaking. That we'd make a plan, *together*.

Wrong.

The only bright side to this day was that by the time we got back, the office was closed. I didn't have to see Bibbi sitting at my table, being all nice and happy.

Oscar walked into the back room right as I was pouring a tea, trying to ignore Hawk as he settled onto the couch.

"How'd it get so dusty in here? Your cleaning crew quit?" Oscar asked two steps in the door.

"We have a dust bunny," Hawk said.

I held back a giggle. A fine layer of dust had already settled on some of the lower shelves, and there were paw prints leading across the wooden floor. Dusty had clearly made herself at home. I'd have to remember her cocoa tomorrow, as I wasn't overly fond of having to live in the dust either, revenge or not.

Oscar dropped onto the other sofa. "Those are the damnedest things to get rid of."

Hawk cleared his throat but didn't say anything else.

"How's the wall?" Oscar asked.

"Holding steady at five," Hawk said.

"What did you think?" Oscar asked me.

As much as I didn't want to discuss this with Hawk, or feed into the delusion that I'd work with him, what I'd just seen was causing a burning need inside of me to talk it over with someone.

I made a noncommittal humming noise. Oscar was easy to find. I'd track him down tomorrow and pick his brain then.

"That's it? No thoughts?" Oscar was still watching and waiting for a response.

I shrugged.

Of course I had thoughts. My wall was cracked. How

could I *not* have thoughts? There were lots of thoughts, including ones for the man staring at me from the couch.

"She doesn't seem to have much to say today," Hawk added, staring as if he could sense how hard it was to keep the words back.

"Any idea on how to fix it yet?" Oscar asked.

I shook my head.

"Doesn't seem like it," Hawk said.

"Why can't she just do another wall? Double it up or something?" Oscar asked, glimpsing over at me before directing his attention to the only person speaking in the room.

"I don't think it will work. Whatever she did the first time I'm not sure she could duplicate. It wasn't the spell we were working on. She's just as likely to tear what is there down completely or make it worse."

"So no new ideas?"

"No, I don't think so. Unless Tippi has something to add?" Hawk asked.

I turned to him. "No. I don't."

"Any ideas?" Oscar asked, alternating his looks between me and Hawk.

I shrugged as I sipped my tea.

Oscar narrowed his eyes on me. "Why aren't you talking?"

Another shrug, because that was not the conversation I was having now.

He didn't waste a second before turning to Hawk. "Why isn't she talking? She's usually feistier than this. I mean, I can see the words wanting to come out, but she's, like, visibly biting her tongue."

Hawk glanced at me. I refused to look back.

He looked at Oscar. "She's mad, and the anger seems to be increasing."

"Was it the apartment?" Oscar looked at me. "I told him not to do it. Said it was a bad move." Oscar dragged a finger across his neck as he shook his head.

I sipped my tea. If I started a list, we'd be here all night.

"Wow. You're so mad you won't even talk about it." Oscar turned back to Hawk. "This is bad."

"I couldn't tell you, since she's not discussing it with me," Hawk said in a glib tone.

"Maybe I should stop by Zark's tomorrow and sit at the bar," Oscar said. "Bet you tell Gregor why you're mad. You two looked chummy enough the last time I stopped by." He got off the couch and moved to sit on the shelves beside me, his shoulder brushing against mine. "Keep flirting with the boy that way and you're going to make me jealous."

I choked on my tea. Oscar had come by for all of five minutes. He'd sat at the bar, and he hadn't looked even slightly jealous. What was he up to now?

Oscar moved closer, flipping a lock of my hair in his fingers. "Unless you're trying to make me jealous? Is that it, doll?"

I wasn't sure what Oscar's game was, but he was shameless at it.

"Did you come by for anything in particular, Oscar?" Hawk said. He was still sitting, but he looked like he wanted to get off the couch and lunge at Oscar.

"Just to see what was up," Oscar said, smiling.

The door to the office opened in the other room.

"It's Bibbi," Hawk said, as if he had some sort of inner alert that told him who was walking into his building.

Bibbi popped her head into the back room and glanced around, her eyes tripping when they hit Hawk. "Hi, all. Just I left my bag here." She held it up as if she needed to prove the reason. "Uh, Hawk, while you're here, could I get your opinion on something in the other room? I was having a problem with one of the slips."

"Sure."

"Well, night," Bibbi said, walking back into the other room. Hawk got up and followed her.

"I'm sorry I always have so many questions and I'm always bothering you," she said, her voice higher than normal, carrying into the back room.

"It's fine," he said.

They were still talking, but their voices were muffled as they got farther into the office. No matter how I angled my head, I couldn't hear what else was being said. What I could hear very well was Oscar's laugh.

Was I that obvious? One look at Oscar said yes.

I dropped my tea onto the table, grabbed my jacket, and headed to the door, nodding to Oscar. I wasn't walking past them to go to my room, and I did want to talk things out.

"Where are you going?"

"I've got some errands to run."

And a lot of aggravation to work out.

17

Two hot cocoas in my hand and I was on my way to Zab's. Whatever he had planned for today was going to be easier than what I'd done all day. I felt like I could barely straighten up after Bautere had handed me my ass all day. Still, I'd stopped for cocoa because I couldn't show up empty-handed with all the help Zab was giving me.

I made a right, only a few minutes from his place when I saw two familiar faces up ahead, Braid and Spike. I would've called after them but was fairly certain that would only make them walk faster. I'd have to chase them down.

Cocoa or info. This should've been an easier choice, but I really did like my cocoa. Still, I needed to know who'd dragged me back here. Were they friend or foe?

I walked as fast as I could to Zab's, put the two cocoas on the stoop, and then ran. They might be lukewarm when I got back, but it would have to do. It was the best compromise possible at the moment.

People stared as I took off down the street. Braid noticed first, seeing the attention I was getting and glancing behind him. He said something to Spike, and then they both ran.

"I just want to talk to you!"

"We have nothing to say!" Spike yelled, as he kept going.

Lucky for me, neither of them were very fast. They were both huffing as I continued to gain on them.

We passed the buildings and were in a field when Braid dropped to his knees, a palm to the ground, dragging in air like his life depended on it.

Spike hesitated for a second, looked at me, looked at Braid again, and then kept running. I let him go. I only needed one, and Braid had seemed the smarter of the two anyway.

I circled until I was leaning over him, a bit short of wind myself.

He put up a hand. "Don't hurt me! It wasn't my fault. I was only doing a job."

"For who?" I asked. Whoever it had been, they'd given him a lofty view of my current abilities.

"I don't know. I got an envelope filled with cash and a warning that you weren't to be harmed."

So, a friend or protective of their assets, like some other people I knew. Not for a second did I think it was Hawk, though. He couldn't wait to get me out of here.

"What else did your instructions say?"

He tried to crawl a few steps away from me, but I followed him. "Nothing. Just that you were very strong and very important. That I should drop you off somewhere in the vicinity of the Sweet Shop before cutting you loose."

That made zero sense, and yet I didn't think he was lying. Braid and Spike were grunt workers. I'd met enough of them at this point to tell. They took orders. They didn't mastermind anything.

"And then what? Someone was going to kill me there?"

"I don't know. I was supposed to just leave you there." He moved back and then fell on his ass.

I pointed my finger at him, jabbing it at the air like I could actually do something on purpose. "Don't lie to me. What else? There had to be something else."

"That's it. I swear!" He put hands together in front of me. "Please, I was just doing a job. I can find the note and show you if you don't kill me." He sniffed suspiciously.

He was telling the truth, or something close, even if it did make zero sense. Whoever had hired him had clearly put the fear of God into him.

"Fine. I believe you, but if I ever find out you lied to me..."

"You won't." He got back on his knees and then fell backward again in his need to scramble away from me, crawling a few feet before getting to his feet. He kept his eyes on me as he circled until he got far enough away to start running again.

If possible, this place just got stranger. I made my way back toward Zab's with no more information than before. Why would someone grab me and drop me off in the middle of the road, right near the Sweet Shop, of all places? An area where I might have some allies? Were they hoping another herd of grouslies would get me?

Zab was standing on his stoop with the two abandoned cocoas. "Have some pressing business?"

"Something like that. Can you heat those up? I always boil them over when I try."

"Already done," he said, handing me back a toasty cup as we walked inside his place.

I tossed my jacket on his couch. "I just saw Braid and Spike. I was trying to get answers about who hired them to bring me back here."

"And?"

"Clueless, as expected. Said they got an envelope with cash and instructions not to hurt me and to drop me off near the Sweet Shop." I sipped my cocoa as his face skewed, probably a mirror image of mine a few minutes ago.

He put his cocoa down as he stared at me, as if I'd have more answers.

When there was no more information forthcoming, he said, "But that makes no sense."

"I know. If it was a setup of some sort to try to sabotage me, why stress that I shouldn't be hurt? Why drop me so close to here and possible allies?"

He took another couple of sips of cocoa before he said, "It almost sounds as if this was someone trying to help you," shaking his head.

"Why not come forward after I'm here?"

He was shaking his head still. Then he squinted and leaned close to my hair.

"What? Is there a bug or something?" I asked, running a hand through my locks.

"No. You're turning, is all," he said, as if I'd have a clue what he was talking about.

"Are you saying I have a grey hair?"

"Looks like a pink one and a turquoise not far from it. Interesting."

"What do you mean?" I didn't wait for him to explain and went to his bathroom, leaning in close to the mirror. He was right. I had weird colors growing in my hair. "What is this? Is it a curse or something?" I asked Zab, who'd followed me in and was looking for more strands of oddness in the back of my head.

"No more a curse than mine. Just happens with some people. Although typically when it happens, it's one color. I guess your magic shines a multitude. Never seen that before."

"You mean you don't dye the tips of your hair blue?"

He laughed. "That would be way too much work. It's just the color it grows, sometimes brighter or paler depending on how much magic I've been using."

"So I'm going to have rainbow hair?" I had to follow him out into the living room because he'd already moved on from his curiosity.

"I don't think so. Looks like just streaks. Mine doesn't turn until it's grown in. Yours looks like it's going to start from the roots, but not all over. It happens to some of us. It's like a genetic thing. Yours should be an interesting look. I don't think I've ever seen that color pattern grow in before."

"How bad do you think it'll get? Do you see any more?" I asked, leaning my head in front of him, forcing him to keep looking.

"Oh, here's a silver that sparkles. That's pretty cool."

I didn't want my hair to sparkle. I didn't want an interesting look. The last person who'd seen me light up like a rainbow had called me evil.

I grabbed the mass of it and twisted it into a bun. "I'm going to have to dye it."

He laughed. "You can't dye it. It won't take. It won't even stick to it."

I leaned both hands on his table. I'd made a decision not to hide anymore, but this felt like I'd be wearing a banner around, screaming to everyone just how different I was, even in the land of different.

He pointed to my hair. "Bun isn't a good idea. You've got some yellow coming in along the hairline in the back."

I yanked the bun out. It was useless and it shouldn't matter. This was who I was. I'd wanted to come back to Xest so I didn't have to hide. Why fight so hard to be here if I was going to act the same way I had my entire life in Salem? If I was going to be that girl, the one who hid, why bother fighting at all? I should just give up now.

"You okay?" Zab asked. "I think it's going to look pretty, but if you'd been hoping for green or something, I can understand the disappointment. I personally would prefer what you have, but we've all got our preferences."

I didn't hide. I would not be that girl anymore.

"No. I'm good with it. It's part of me, and that's okay."

"I think it's going to be hot."

I refused to toy with my hair even as Zab kept looking at it.

"It really is interesting how you've got a multitude of colors, though. Seriously. I've never seen that."

"Yeah, interesting. So what are we working on today?" I was more than ready to move on to a new subject.

"Oh, uh, some charms." He pointed to the pile of crystals, furry-feet-looking things, twigs twisted into the shape of people, and stuff I couldn't put a name to. "Good-luck charm or bad luck? Pick your poison."

"Good luck. *Definitely* good luck." I wasn't going anywhere near a bad-luck charm. I was quite capable of handling that one on my own.

18

"You're not paying attention," Bautere said.

"I can honestly say I was doing the best I possibly could." I was flat on my back in the snow for the fifteenth time. No one did this on purpose.

"You'd be dead if you were fighting for real," he said, ending on a growl.

"Isn't this why you're training me?" I asked, sitting up and then getting to my feet again. "Wouldn't it be better if we focused on using some magic? I've never been good at combat sports."

Getting pushed to the ground over and over again wasn't what I'd thought I was signing up for. If I was going to become kickass by pure physical standards, I was going to need another ten years.

"What do you think we're doing?" he growled.

The growls didn't have the same effect they used to after you'd heard a good twenty.

"I'm supposed to be using magic?" He was not the trainer I'd hoped for, that was definite. Was there another Bautere around I could talk to?

"When your magic becomes one with every movement you make, then you'll be ready," he said, getting in the crouching position that told me I was going to be crashing into the snow again.

"How do I do that?" I asked, crouching, waiting for his attack.

"You visualize it. You let the magic flow through you. You don't try to control it. You are it. It is you."

"What if it doesn't want to be me and I can't seem to make it?" I was squeezing in every free moment to practice with him, even when that meant almost no sleep. "My magic doesn't like to do what it's supposed to."

"Then you practice until it does."

It all sounded good. Somehow I was supposed to be able to leap over his back as he lunged for me. Then hit him from overhead as I landed.

I tried to let the magic flow freely through my body. And when he lunged, I crashed into the snow on the side.

A few hours later, I sipped on something that tasted like tequila as I stood behind the bar at Zark's. It wouldn't fix the soreness of my muscles and bruises, but it would make me forget about them for a while.

It was only an hour into my shift when Hawk strolled into the place, walked up to the bar, and said, "We need to go somewhere."

The line of his jaw told me that whatever this was about, it wasn't good.

"I can't just leave. I'm working." Even if my working was standing in the vicinity of Gregor as he served most of the drinks. It was still a paycheck.

"Zark, Tippi's done for the day," Hawk said, not breaking eye contact with me. "Shall I get your jacket, or would you like to?"

I was well aware we had a crowd listening in, because as we talked, they didn't. Gregor also inched closer. I shook my head, telling him I had this under control.

Gregor didn't back up, but he also didn't pursue it. We'd already done this rodeo once before. He knew the ropes.

"I have a job to do," I said to Hawk with steel laced in my tone. This was it. This was the hill I would die on. He would not take control of my life again. If that meant an all-out brawl in the middle of Zark's with an audience, then that was the way it was going to happen.

A hand holding my jacket shot out in front of me.

"Here you go. See you tomorrow," Zark said. "Best be on your way."

Okay, maybe this wasn't the hill I'd die on, since the owner of said hill seemed to be pushing me down it. But that hill was coming. Seemed there were hills all around me, just waiting for someone to die, and that would be me. Just not today, maybe.

I took my coat as Hawk smiled.

I didn't ask what Hawk wanted until we got outside. And then he was too far ahead of me to ask. I looked back at Zark's, knowing I'd only get shown the door again if I attempted to go back. I looked down the street, toward the broker's office, debating on going there. But then I'd have to watch Bibbi working at my table. Might as well follow him and find out what he wanted, since work was done for the day.

"Keep up," he said, not bothering to look back or realize that maybe I wasn't keeping up for a reason. The more space, the better. He was testy, I was angry, and together we were on the brink of something much worse.

I wasn't going to ask him what his problem was because it was his, not mine. As soon as I asked, I'd take ownership on some level. That was what always happened when I asked about someone else's problem. It was like buying stock in a company that you knew was about to nosedive, and I wasn't doing it. He could be as quiet as he wanted and hold it all in, the way he probably preferred.

He kept moving at his pace, and I continued at mine in the direction of the wall. Not sure why we were walking the whole way, but I wasn't asking about that either. If he had to wait for me to catch up once he got there, then he waited. I wasn't his employee. I was here because I chose to help, and he'd have to deal with that whatever way I chose to do it.

He stopped again, further up the hill, watching me move at my slower pace, as if his steely stare would speed me up.

Not.

They must've put salt in his morning cocoa the way he was acting. All the shit he'd done to me, and here he was with the attitude and no explanation.

I passed him on the hill, wondering when he was going to decide to walk again but not really caring. I could go look at the cracks myself, and there were definitely either new ones or worsened ones. The feeling of dread hadn't been this bad here yesterday.

I got to the wall, and there it was. You didn't need to run a hand over this one to see how badly it was breaking. One side jutted out several more inches than the other.

I laid a hand on the break anyway, trying to feel for something, a way to heal it or a magical signature. Anything.

"How does this keep happening?" I asked, not specifically talking to Hawk. He didn't have any answers either.

"I think it's sabotage," Hawk said, answering anyway. "Feel over here," he said, pointing five feet away. "There's a strange feeling."

I did as he suggested. Any other place I laid my hand, I would either feel my magic or its magic. This was different. There wasn't even a clear signal, more of a muddy feeling.

I looked up at him, the question obvious on my face.

"That's what it feels like when someone is disguising their mark," he said.

"Six. If it is them, they're making ground and we're losing it." I took a couple of steps back, taking the whole of this newer one in, standing shoulder to shoulder with Hawk.

"Come on. Let's check the rest."

We made the rest of the rounds in silence, coming to a truce of sorts. Hawk and I had our differences, but with this, we were one hundred percent in sync. Our feud was shed the moment we got here.

As we finished, I saw a door waiting in the distance. Our short moment of peace seemed to be going away.

He waited beside it. "Are you coming, or do you have somewhere else to be?"

"I'll gladly take the shortcut, thank you." I walked into the hall of the broker building before I added, "This gets me closer to where I need to be. I have plans for the evening."

His eyes narrowed on me with a level of heat I'd not yet seen directed my way.

I walked downstairs a little faster than normal, hitting the landing and heading into the offices and then the back room instead. If he was going to pursue this fight, I'd rather do it here, where there was a door, than in my bedroom.

When he didn't immediately follow, I thought it was over, that he'd left. Good.

I was sipping tea on the couch when Hawk walked in and decided to stand a few feet in front of me. It was his dictator pose, one I was all too familiar with. I continued to drink my tea, pretending I wasn't sitting in the shadow of his looming self.

"I can't have someone on my team that can't defend themselves. I can't even leave to handle things without you disappearing when half of Xest wants you dead."

It would've been all too easy to tell him I was working on how to defend myself. Several big issues, though. It wasn't any of his business. There was no way I'd tell him just to end a fight. If I gave in and told him about my secret training, then what? He'd think he was entitled to know everything I did?

And come to think of it, what did he know about my disappearing?

"Do you have people tracking me or something? I didn't know I was supposed to report every single place I went to you. Now that I know, I'll make *sure* I still don't do it."

"You're not listening. You don't realize what some of these people will do." He leaned forward, putting one hand on the arm of the couch and the other on the back, effectively forcing me backward unless I wanted to end up hugging him.

"Because I don't have to listen to you. Also, I'm not on your team. And second, you're crowding me."

"If you could defend yourself, I wouldn't be able to crowd you. I wouldn't have to force you back here. I wouldn't have to worry about you dying every time you walked out the door."

He made it sound all so chivalrous, just a man worried about someone he cared for. But I knew better now, knew how quickly he used and then discarded people. I'd been fooled by the caring act too many times before.

I pushed on his chest. "I'm starting to think that you don't want me to learn anything. You like being able to torture me."

His gaze was on my lips. His leg was bent, resting in between mine, and damned if I didn't wish he'd bring it forward, just a couple of inches, because even though I shouldn't want him, there was no denying that I did.

There was something very right and very wrong about our chemistry. Or the way I felt alive when he was around. I'd spent too many years hiding out in Salem, and now my body went crazy anytime it got adrenaline. I should be swinging at him right now, and I was wetting my lips instead.

"I guess that's one way to describe your relationship. Not sure I've even seen quite this mode of torture," Oscar said, laughing as he walked past us. I hadn't even heard him walk in.

Hawk straightened. I readjusted myself, feeling like a kid who'd just gotten caught doing something bad. Not that I would've actually done anything, so I was not sure what my problem was. Just because an attractive male got close, it didn't mean it was my fault I was attracted to him on a cellular level.

I stood and, with an awkward nod to Oscar, made my exit.

19

It had been so sunny, but the minute I stepped outside the broker's office, it was as if a storm cloud, a dark, mean one, hovered overhead. It was too cold to rain in Xest, but it looked like it would be one hell of a snow day. I picked up my pace, hurrying to Zark's before this thing unloaded on me. The cloud was drifting the same way I was walking, but I luckily made it to Zark's before it dumped its foul weather onto me.

I tucked my bag away under the bar.

Gregor was already there, giving me a smile. "Beautiful day, huh?"

"It was, but not so much now. Looks like there's a storm about to let loose."

"Really? I didn't see that coming. Oh well. So what have you been up to? How's it going over at the broker house?" He came over and leaned on the bar next to where I was standing.

"It's okay. Not the worst. I'm sure you've heard all the gossip, but it's not as bad as all that." The way people stared at Hawk, if I didn't downplay it a bit, they'd imagine he was about to murder me.

"Yeah, I've noticed you hold your own with him."

"Not that big of a deal. I swear." I grabbed the towel off the bar, looking for something to wipe down or anything other than this conversation. Gregor was a nice guy, but when he looked at me like I walked on water, it was a bit much to swallow.

He followed me as I worked my way along the bar top. "You know, I've been meaning to ask if you want to go get that..."

Zark slammed the door open, walked in, and gave the crowd a stare-down. "Who brought the black cloud? You know that's not allowed here. You have a black cloud, you stay home or go somewhere else."

He scanned the crowd.

No one spoke.

I leaned closer to Gregor and whispered, "What's he mean by brought the black cloud? Clouds just happen... don't they?"

"That cloud you saw when you got here, someone must have brought it when they came. Maybe they thought your good luck would rub off on them."

"You mean that cloud that is overhead right now isn't bad weather?" The one that seemed to be moving with me for my walk. Oh, no. I saw where this one was heading, and I wasn't going down because it wasn't a sunny day. Not this time.

"A black cloud doesn't move like a normal cloud, not even for the fifth wind. It follows a particular person, and it's easy to spot because it seems to stagnate over a person no matter where the wind is blowing."

"Speak up!" Zark said loudly. "Who brought the black

cloud, and don't lie. It's been hovering over here for ten minutes already."

Gregor's brows dropped as he looked my way. He wasn't the only one. Most of the people in the room were starting to look at me too. It was like a contagion that was spreading until all eyes landed on me. Someone might've come in right before me. Maybe they'd been walking here a few minutes in front of me? It was possible. It wasn't necessarily me.

Zark followed everyone else's gaze and settled on me, the lines on his face growing deeper by the second. He crossed the room.

A clap of thunder rang out so loud that it felt like the building shook. One of the regulars I knew by face got up and started edging his way toward the door, as if hoping no one would notice.

Zark saw him. I saw him. The entire room saw him.

It *couldn't* have been me. I was good luck. Everyone thought I was. Was everyone wrong? For once, I was the beacon of light? Right?

Zark looked around again and then back to me.

"Tippi, can I have a word with you?"

"Yeah, sure."

Another customer, this one near the far wall, headed toward the bathroom. There was a back door in that direction. It was such an obvious ploy. I didn't even bat an eye when he quickly dodged to the exit instead.

I walked around the bar, thinking we'd go in the back to talk.

Zark walked toward the door. "We should talk out there," he said.

He opened the door and waited. Outside, the darkness

of the cloud loomed overhead and ate up our shadows. Everywhere else, the sun was shining.

"Let's walk a ways down the street. I don't want patrons listening in." He was looking up as he said it.

He walked to the end of the building and waited. Okay, that wasn't that far. He'd be hard-pressed to notice a change that slight, even if he was staring upward with an eagle eye. But if he wanted to go any farther, I was going to have to fake an ankle injury. I couldn't lose this job. Not with immigration looming. And to lose it over a storm cloud? That was insane. We were probably going to be buried in snow soon, and I'd be out of work? No. I wasn't taking the hit for bad weather.

I made my way to him, avoiding looking up.

He was, though.

"Tippi, maybe you should take the day. I don't want any of this nasty business sullying your reputation." He made a shooing motion, as if trying to get me away from the building as fast as he could without touching me.

"That's not my cloud. I should probably stay." I didn't have a black cloud. It was bad weather. If I left and it cleared, it would be my cloud forevermore. What if I left and a gust of wind pushed it along with me? My reputation would be sullied in all of Xest, and I couldn't take another hit in that department.

"No, no, you should go and rest up." He inched forward, still trying to shoo me. "You should take the night off—full pay, of course. I insist. You look tired, and you don't need this additional stress."

There were only two choices: (A) walk away with some dignity, or (B) refuse, run back into the bar, and have them drag me out while I left nail marks in my wake. It was tempting for sure.

"Okay. Maybe you're right." I nodded for a few seconds, not moving as I looked upward. "I'll see you tomorrow, though, right? I come in for my shift?"

"Of course." He nodded, but not vigorously. It was a little bounce, like his chin had hit a speed bump it was forced to get over.

I edged a few feet away, walking backward, nodding and waving at Zark as he watched.

He hadn't taken a step toward the door. He was standing and watching me, smiling and waving back, as if enjoying the shade of the dark cloud above.

I had to move. If I didn't, I'd look like I thought it was my cloud. Maybe if I walked very slowly. I crossed the street and made my way down the block at a pace that would lose to a turtle. I didn't look up until I was a mile away. I didn't need to. I knew it was still over me by the brightness of the street ahead of me and the lack of shadow where I walked. Still, I glanced up. There it was. The black cloud. I turned around and looked back toward Zark's. The sun was shining brightly. I looked ahead to nothing but sunny skies.

The only place the sun wouldn't shine was over me.

Shit. It *was* mine.

Bautere was staring upward as I approached.

"You've got a dark cloud," he said as I neared.

"It's not mine." It didn't matter what anyone said; I wasn't claiming this thing. No way.

"It came with you."

"I don't care. It's not mine," I said, walking to the

center of the clearing. "Why? Are you afraid of practicing with me?"

I'd hiked up here first thing this morning, just to be out of the broker building before the sun broke and the black cloud became obvious. Now even the great Bautere didn't want to come near me. I'd wander around the wall next, not that I knew what to do about that either.

Bautere laughed deeply. "No, you'd have to bring something a lot darker than that cloud to scare me. Are you ready?"

"I'm here, aren't I?" Was I ready? I was never really ready. Wasn't sure I ever would be. That was the problem.

He crouched and then lunged at me.

I shot up at the last second, soaring a good ten feet in the air. Instead of rotating in midair, I fell again, crashing into the snow and rolling to a stop.

I sat up and smiled. I'd failed again. But not completely. For a moment there, I'd felt like I was flying. Black cloud be damned. I could do this. I *was* going to do this.

"Looks like the witch is finally learning to wield her magic," Bautere said

"I guess I am." I got to my feet, ready to try again.

———

I weaved through another alley, making my way to Zark's without an audience. After how much progress I'd made at practice, I'd walk out of this alley, and the sun would shine down on me. And if it didn't, it was because it wasn't shining on anyone. There was no way I still had a black cloud lingering.

The first step wasn't good. Nor were the next ten or twenty. It was sunny everywhere but where I walked.

It would go away. I'd keep walking and it would disappear. Walking was even easier today, as I was clearing the way like I was Hawk. No one wanted to get anywhere near me.

I got to Zark's a few minutes later. The place was empty. It was the same shift I always worked, but something was definitely different. Even if the place had been packed, I'd have known something was wrong with Zark as soon as I walked in. His smile, normally lit from the reflection off all the coin he was bringing in, was dimmed.

Gregor was smiling. He glanced at his father and smiled wider, as if he could balance out the vibe in the empty bar.

"Tippi, we need to talk," Zark said.

I tucked my hands in my pockets and nodded. I couldn't take the look on his face for too long. The flat eyes that didn't sparkle with coins.

"I know. It's the cloud." There was no more denying it. I had a cloud.

"You know, sometimes it's a fluke and they hang on to the wrong person for a little bit before they realize the mistake," Gregor said.

Zark didn't acknowledge him. "I saw it heading this way with you. Who knows how long it might last? I can't afford to have it here."

"I get it." I kept nodding, not sure what else to do or say. I couldn't blame him or even be mad. What else could you do with a person haunted by a black cloud? This place had never been so empty.

"I can pay you to leave if you want?"

I shook my head and took a step back. "No, that won't be needed."

I was fired. What did you say when you got fired?

Zark didn't know what else to say either, as he started bobbing his head as well. Or he knew exactly what to say but didn't have the nerve to tell me to get out because of who I was associated with. Looked like I was going to have to kick myself out.

I hooked a thumb toward the door. "I guess I'll get going."

"If it goes away, stop by. Maybe I can hire you back." He lifted a shoulder and scratched his jaw, as if it weren't beyond impossible.

I smiled, as if that made me feel so much better.

I waved toward Gregor, who wouldn't want to have anything to do with me either.

I was only a couple steps outside of Zark's when Gregor called my name and chased after me.

"Hey, I hope you know this doesn't affect our friendship at all, right?"

Even as he spoke, people were crossing the street to get away from me. I hadn't thought we were actually friends, but I couldn't afford to lose any right now, especially with the list of fifty I needed for immigration. It was bad enough I'd just lost my job.

Another wave of people parted as they approached us. Still...

"You sure?"

Gregor waved toward the people giving us a wide berth. "Definitely. Black clouds happen to everyone at some point."

They did? Then why was everyone acting so weird? "You've had a black cloud?"

He tucked his hands in his pockets, looking around the now-empty street. "Uhm, well, not really. I'm sure I will at some point." He ducked his head, and then shrugged before looking at me. "Even if I don't, I don't care if you do."

"Thanks." With a sea of people running from me, it was nice to have someone not ebbing and flowing with the tide. He wasn't a bad-looking guy, and he just got a little cuter.

"Can I come by and say hi sometime? We're friends, right? I'd hate to think we'd never hang out again."

"Definitely." Black cloud or not, I felt a little less bleak.

"Maybe a cocoa tomorrow night?"

"Sure." How could I turn down a guy that was so set on being loyal to me?

20

I walked Xest for a good hour, trying to shake the dark cloud, before I gave up. The broker's office was silent as I walked in—until the monkeys started their funeral procession music to the beat of my step. They'd been practicing that one—a lot. They didn't need the directive to stop this time. Once glance did the job.

Zab smiled, but it was the pitying variety. Bibbi was giving me straight-up pity, sans the smile to water it down. My situation was so bad that apparently pity had outranked fear.

Musso glanced up and looked around the room and then back at me. "So she got fired? So she's got a black cloud? Not the end of the world." He grunted and went back to work.

"You all know." Who needed a newsflash paper when gossip traveled at the speed of light?

"Zark posted a sign on his door that you were gone and it was safe to come back about a half an hour ago," Musso said.

"So you got fired?" Zab asked.

I dropped into Belinda's old seat, afraid to get too close to anyone in case it was catchy. "Yep. The tides seem to be turning. I was good luck, and now I'm bad. So bad that he offered to continue to pay me to stay away. It was too humiliating to accept."

Although I'd thought of it, right after, the thought of food occurred to me. In the end, the shame of getting paid to stay away beat out hunger, especially when there were usually crackers or rolls at the tea station here. Wasn't sure if that logic would hold up after eating nothing but crackers for a month. Looked like I'd find out. At least there was no rent to pay, but that would probably change too if this black cloud didn't go away.

"How does a person even end up with a black cloud?" I asked the room in general.

Musso shrugged, not bothering to look up from his work. "It happens. You probably did something you didn't even realize."

"Did you open an umbrella inside?" Zab asked.

"Or spill salt that wasn't being used in a puddle?" Bibbi asked.

"Break a mirror? That would do it for sure," Zab said.

The monkeys broke into something suspiciously close to a murder-mystery theme song. They were getting better. If their timing wasn't so horrendous, I might appreciate it.

"Not. Now."

Their playing screeched to a halt, literally.

"Always suppressed. We're artists. We need to express ourselves," Speak No Evil said.

I ignored the glares coming from the band and turned back to Zab and Bibbi, since Musso had already moved on. "I didn't do any of those things."

Zab started drumming his pencil on his desk. "Well, they do sometimes just spontaneously appear. It could've happened by pure dumb luck."

"Are bad things going to start happening now?" I waved a hand. "Forget I asked that. I just got fired. That's obviously not a good thing."

I slumped forward, my forehead in my hand. That was when the silence hit me. The black cloud had followed me here. Had it scared all the people away?

I squinted an eye open. "Why is it so empty here? Has it been empty all day?"

So much for not paying rent. I might be homeless *and* jobless soon. I felt something invisible and furry brush against my hand right before a wet tongue licked my nose. Even Dusty pitied me.

Bibbi started fidgeting and suddenly needed to go into the back room. Musso was following her before she was out of the room, mumbling about how she messed up the tea station every time she touched anything. Zab watched them leave like they'd taken off with the last lifeboat on the *Titanic*.

"Zab?"

He stopped drumming his pencil as if he'd given up the fight. "We were busy, but not overly so. Probably just a lag about this time."

Musso walked back into the office. Now that he'd handled the tea problem, he'd give me a straight answer.

"Musso, was it busy before I showed up?"

Without a pause in his step, he said, "The place was packed until someone saw you. They came in and said, 'The Nowhere witch is heading this way and she's still got the cloud.' We cleared out in under two minutes."

"I should leave. I don't want to ruin business for you guys too. It's bad enough I emptied out Zark's."

"Don't worry about it, kid. I needed the time to catch up. I'm way behind with paperwork." Musso settled back in at his desk.

"And you know I don't care," Zab said.

"Neither do I—if you care, that is," Bibbi said, poking her head out of the back room.

Bibbi was turning out to be impossible to hate. If she could go work somewhere else, though, it would make not hating her so much easier. Every time she sat at my table, I had to force myself not to drag her outside.

"Thanks, Bibbi. I do care," I said, and mostly meant it because I wasn't a monster. It wasn't her fault that Hawk had made her the big usurper.

I sank another couple inches into Belinda's seat, wishing that there was a hole in the floor that would gobble me up.

"Is there anything I can do to get rid of it?" I asked.

"No," Musso said.

Zab shook his head. Bibbi looked as clueless as me. Yeah, it was very hard to hate someone who knew less than I did.

Luckily, we'd fallen silent right before Hawk walked in the office. He probably knew everything already, but I couldn't bear having this discussion in front of him.

Before I'd gotten back to Xest, I'd daydreamed of coming to this office, walking up to Hawk, and not having to say a word. Success would be written all over me. I'd reek of it. I'd be dressed in the best Xest fashions. I'd have a killer place near the square and I'd be all around rocking this existence. I'd have found my way here in spite of him.

The reality wasn't quite as nice. I was slumped in a chair in his office, staring at my replacement across the way. I'd been recently fired, forced to live here again, and half my wardrobe was still hand-me-down clothes picked out by Belinda.

He'd even boot me now. Would he tell me to get my apartment back? Where would I go? Could I get another place with this cloud hanging over my head? I didn't want to be here, but getting kicked to the curb twice, first from my job and then from my room? I wasn't sure I was up to that either. Perhaps I should try to sneak upstairs out of sight for a while.

No. That would be hiding, and I didn't do that anymore. Good thing I remembered before I snuck away.

Hawk crossed the room, not saying anything about the emptiness of the place. He picked up a pile of slips and flipped through them.

There was no way he'd missed the cloud when he walked in. There was even less chance he hadn't been told about it. I could sit here and pretend there wasn't an issue or hit it head-on. Considering "head-on" was my new motto, why change tactics now? Might as well go down in a ball of flames. No job, homeless, black cloud—bring it on.

"Well? Do you want me gone? Should I pack my bags or what? Speak now."

Zab and Musso, who'd only been half paying attention to their work, were now fully invested in our conversation. Bibbi actually squeaked. The monkeys decided this was the time to kick back into theme music with a little *duh, duh, duuuuhn* in case we weren't all aware of what was at stake. They apparently thought this was a game show.

Hawk's stone face broke into a smile. Clearly, he hadn't

noticed the theme music graciously provided by the monkeys, because he thought we were in a comedy.

"Why? Because of the black cloud following you everywhere?"

The gleam in his eye and his soft laugh felt like a bucket of salt being poured over road rash. I was glad that my life going to shit brought him such amusement.

"You know what, forget it. I'll go get my bag. I didn't want to be here anyway." Screw him and this place. He'd forced me back, and now he'd laugh as I left? He could go to hell, and now that I knew that place probably existed, I felt a little better about how things might end up.

I moved to the door.

"Tippi," Zab said, getting half out of his chair.

"Stay out of it, Zab. Hawk will handle it," Musso told him.

Hawk handled it by getting to the door first. Great, now he wasn't even going to let me get my things?

I crossed my arms. "I have to get my bag."

"For what? You're not moving out." His words might've sounded bossy, but I liked this Hawk better. At least the smile was gone and the gleam had been buffed out of existence.

I gave him a short nod, acknowledging his words. There would be no thank you or gratefulness forthcoming. I would not get suckered in by his false kindness, not again. No way. Not after he'd screwed me over so many times. He'd get back in my good graces, use me up, and then toss me aside in a heartbeat. You might as well write *sucker* on my forehead if I fell for it.

"It's your building. Your choice if you want to lose customers," I said, daring him to kick me out, because I must've been insane.

"I don't care if people don't come in. They'll come back eventually—or not." He stood there, putting on such a good act that Bibbi sighed. I wouldn't fall for it.

I nodded again before I made my way to the other side of the room, where it was safer. The more distance from him, the better.

I sat at Belinda's now-empty desk again, wishing I could feel happier about having a place to live and less preoccupied with dissecting why that was. If Hawk was at least upfront, it would be an easier pill to swallow than this horse pill of BS he was handing over. He should save the nice act for someone who was buying it, maybe for Bibbi. The way she was staring at him now, she'd buy any load of garbage he sold her.

He followed me over, stared at the desk I was sitting at, then pointed at it. "If you're unemployed, you might as well fill the empty spot."

Bibbi might be a little dippy from the looks of her, but she *had* filled the spot. Talk about just discarding people. The girl was sitting right there while he gave her job away. From the look on her face, she was as traumatized as she should be about it. Poor idiot.

"You hired someone, remember?" I asked, looking at Bibbi and then him. "There is no job available."

Even if it had been my job first, I wouldn't kick her out, no matter how I'd fantasized about it.

He didn't look at Tippi. "She's a sorter. I'm talking about being a broker."

Bibbi sagged in relief.

I was too stunned to do anything. From what I'd heard, being a broker here was about as good a job as you could land. You made all the wheeling and dealings *happen*. Every person in Xest treated the brokers with a certain deference because they could make or break your livelihood. They handed out the best jobs for the most money. It was a dream job.

That he would have control of. That he could take away on a whim. It would be handing him over another part of my life to control so he could screw me, as he had in the past. I would be a masochist to even consider it. It was a nice thought for all of one minute.

"I'm not interested in working for you. I'll find a position of a more permanent nature on my own," I said, crossing my arms and staring him dead in the eye, using all my past grievances to shore up my refusal.

There was a flicker in his eyes, a split second where they shifted away before hardening and meeting my gaze again. "Who said it couldn't be permanent?"

Had to give him credit: he never gave up, ever. If he wanted something, he kept at it. Too bad he hadn't wanted me to stay in Xest.

"The fact that you're the one offering it says it all."

"Mull it over a bit and get back to me," he said, as if I hadn't already said no several times.

He walked into the back room without waiting for another no.

Zab got up and walked over to me. "Are you crazy? Do you know how many people want this position? We make a ton of coin. You'd be set. Everyone would be nice to you. Even the people sneering at you now would probably back off, because everyone wants to work with us."

I glanced at the door, making sure Hawk had stayed in the back room.

"What's the point? So he can take it away whenever he wants? I get comfortable and then he screws me over again, and I hate myself for taking anything from him? No.

I can't do it. I won't work for him." I was crossing my arms again and shaking my head.

"Then you do it for a couple weeks, maybe a month, and quit on your terms, but it'll give you a cushion. Not to mention, if people see you working here, they won't be afraid to hire you if you leave."

Everything he said made sense. It added up neatly in a little row with no errors, except for the rage inside me that Hawk would have that much control over my life. His stamp of approval could make or break me every day.

"I won't give him that kind of control over me again. Not after what happened. I can't do it. It's bad enough I'm back living here. He doesn't get to control my entire life."

"Not even if it's the smart thing to do and you know it?" Zab took a seat on the desk beside me and said, barely above a whisper, "You can't go to immigration with no job."

Shit. I'd been so mad and flustered that I'd forgotten about that little issue hanging over my head. And by little, I meant gigantic. And by hanging over my head, I meant like a guillotine with a worn rope. I didn't want to do it, but was I stupid enough to say no? I might be.

"What if I take it and then he fires me right before? Maybe he was doing this on purpose to screw me?" That would be much more likely than this nice-guy act. Hawk had said himself that he wasn't a nice guy.

Musso cleared his throat and walked over. "Here's what you need to do. We all know this job is your best solution right now. I also understand. He burned you. So you need to get a little insurance. Have Zab negotiate a contract where Hawk can't fire you for a set period of time and make him swear to it so he can't renege."

The monkeys kicked back in, but this time talking like they were sportscasters.

"What do you think she'll do? Will she take the play?" Speak No Evil said in a hushed voice of a commentator with a microphone.

Where had they gotten a pink, glittery microphone? There was probably some little kid out there somewhere crying over a lost karaoke machine.

"It's hard to say. She's been down this road before. Maybe she'll fake to the left and then scramble at the last minute," Hear No Evil said.

"One thing to be said for sure, she'll come out fighting. She's a tough player," See No Evil said.

I looked over. "Not the time for this. Learn to read your crowd.

"Duly noted," Hear No Evil said. "We were trying a new possible avenue. You know, something we've been discussing behind the scenes for entertainment value, since we're working on tips—"

"Shut. Up."

"Got it." Hear No Evil turned off the microphone before saying to the other two, "I don't think this is playing well to the crowd."

I focused back on Musso, ignoring the monkeys who seemed intent on narrating my life story.

"He couldn't break the contract?" I asked.

"Contracts here aren't like the ones in Rest. You swear to something and you're going to hold up to that, whether you want to or not. You'll have some control back, and that's really the problem, isn't it, kid? You want some ownership of your life?"

I bit my lip, thinking it over. Initially, it didn't seem like that was the issue, but the idea of security did wipe away some feelings of anger about the situation. Maybe it was the issue.

"Well? What do you think? Would that work for you?" Zab asked.

You could nearly smell the excitement pouring off him. Even if I'd wanted to play hard to get, one look at the joy in his eyes and it was tough to say no. Bottom line was that I wanted this too. This place still felt like home to me, even if I didn't *want* it to. Knowing I had a secure job on the day I went to immigration? That would save me in so many ways.

"Yeah, okay, if there's a solid contract in place, it could work. If he agrees to that, I can too."

I'd barely finished speaking before Zab ran into the other room.

"You're being smart." Musso gave me the nod, the one he reserved for these types of moments.

"He still has to agree."

"He will." Musso laughed as he walked back to his desk.

Bibbi was giving me nervous smiles from across the room, holding up crossed fingers.

"Thanks," I said, feeling like I didn't want to kill her quite as much as she sat at my table. I mean, if I had this desk, it would be greedy to not let her have the table.

Musso was back to working as if everything would work out as planned.

"Tippi," Hawk called from the back room. He sounded like himself, so it was hard to judge the reception to the contract. Musso nodded as I walked in back, as if encouraging me not to be stupid.

The monkeys marked my steps with drumbeats before trying to fall into step behind me.

I put up a hand to stop them. "You're not coming, and I don't need a theme song for every act of my life. If you don't cut it out, I'm going to step on your instruments, and you'll have to go find another kid to make cry."

They made faces and whispered horrible things. But I walked away in silence.

Zab was glancing back and forth between Hawk and me as I walked in the back.

He rubbed his palms on his hips as he said, "Hawk's got a couple questions, but he's not averse to a contract."

"I can take it from here, Zab," Hawk said, nodding and tilting his head toward the door.

Zab glanced my way, and I nodded as well. If things went badly, I'd rather have no witnesses if I went ballistic. Plus, I didn't need any help. I'd been around the block a few times with Hawk. I could hold my own, mostly.

"If you two think you've got this..." Zab took a very slow step toward the door, waiting for a cry of help before taking another.

"Thanks, Zab. We can handle it," I said.

"I believe you." It took another full minute before he finally made his way out of the room.

Then there were two. I turned toward Hawk with my best poker face. Negotiation time was upon us, and I couldn't afford to lose this one.

"What were your questions?"

His eyes flickered from my face to my arm and then back. "Where did you get that bruise?"

Shit. I'd pushed my sleeves up without realizing it. Figured he'd notice. If Hawk were a normal person, I'd be able to tell him I was practicing defense with Bautere. Hawk was anything but normal. He'd have a gazillion questions, and then he'd have a list of what I was doing wrong and what I needed to do. So instead of being honest, telling him I was training to be a kickass witch, I'd let him think I was an idiot.

"I banged into the door when the lights were out."

He leaned his hip on the shelf, crossing his arms. "That's an odd shape for a door."

I leaned on the back of the couch. "I stumbled into the dresser afterward. Was that your question?"

"Not quite. I've never lied to you, but my word isn't good enough for you to take the job?"

He had me there, and I wasn't sure I could say the same. Wow. Even that was a lie. I *knew* I couldn't say the same. I'd lied to him more than once. The only difference was that in our previous relationship, he hadn't *had* to lie. He'd called all the shots. I'd been powerless and wouldn't willingly walk into that situation again.

"I'm not saying you have, but I want guarantees. I know how fickle you can be."

"Fickle?" He nodded a couple times, and the little vein on his neck bulged for a second or two.

It warmed my cold heart for some reason.

"Yes, I'd say fickle is the right term."

"Fine. If you'd like a contract, that can be arranged. It might be better for both of us, since your agreements have a tendency to be flexible in nature. You like to renegotiate on a whim. This way, we both know where we stand."

"She was going to die in that factory." Of course he'd bring up my trying to free Rabbit. I should've expected it after I'd called him fickle.

"I understand what you were doing, but then again, I can be fickle, so an iron-clad contract is definitely for the best." He crossed his arms before he continued, "I swear that I won't fire you..." He kept talking, and the next words were incoherent until he stopped, looked at me, and said, "Now you accept," in an over-enunciated, arrogant manner.

"What were those weird words in the middle?"

"You wanted a contract. I gave you one. If you were practicing with me still, you'd know exactly what I said."

"Translate it." I had a feeling that his mumbled words were the equivalent of the small print in a written contract.

"It means you get what you want. You can stay here as long as you choose. If you don't want to accept it, then don't." His complete indifference as to whether I accepted felt like a little horde of bees attacking my ego.

"Answer me one question first: did you have something to do with the black cloud?"

"If I did, I'd tell you. No one even knows where they come from or how they form. You can go through every spell book in Xest and not find a reliable spell for one."

I believed him. He would admit it. He had no shame. He'd screw you over ten times to Tuesday and then put it on a bulletin board for the world to see.

"Are you satisfied? Because I do have other things to do today besides begging you to take one of the best jobs in Xest." He walked away from me after a split-second wait to make himself a tea, putting it in a cup that I knew he liked to take with him. He was leaving. That would be it. I was sure these contracts didn't dangle in the air forever. There had to be some expiration, and I had immigration looming. If this backfired somehow, I'd figure it out after I got the three hags off my back.

"I accept."

I felt a swoosh of air around the room.

He turned to me. "It's done. Zab and Musso will show you the ropes."

My blood was pumping so hard that I could barely hear past the buzzing in my ears. This wasn't exactly what I'd planned, but it was a good job, in a place I loved, even if the words burned on the tongue. I had some security now.

He walked out the back door, as if it were nothing.

I walked into the office. The monkeys took one look at my face and lifted their instruments. They broke into "She's a Dandy," and I didn't even want to crush their little drum set.

The room smiled at me—even Bibbi looked happy that things were working out. We might be able to be friends now that the bitterness was washed away a bit.

"I guess you're back to work," Zab said, getting out of his chair.

"Temporarily." I was actively fighting the urge to skip around the office, and it hurt my cheeks to keep the smile off my face. This was not a permanent situation. This was a necessity only. There could be no celebrating.

"This definitely deserves a cocoa," Zab said. "Musso? Bibbi?"

"Place is empty. Might as well," Musso said.

"Definitely," Bibbi said.

Well, it was a cocoa, and I couldn't very well not go when it was for me. Plus, I'd started a list of names for immigration references, and what better time to hit up Gilli, the owner? And maybe a couple of her employees, too?

Zab held the door open for me. "Feels a little like old times, doesn't it?"

I was afraid to agree with him as I walked out the door.

I took a step outside, and the sun was shining down on me, my shadow as crisp as ever. Just like that, I had my shadow back. The black cloud had disappeared.

"It's gone," I said, looking overhead.

Zab was squinting in my direction.

"Why are you looking at me like there's something off? This is good."

Zab shook his head. "No, not the cloud. I just..." He was looking at me this way and that. "I don't know exactly. Maybe it's just a residue from the deal. Musso?"

Musso took a good look at me. "There's something there, but it's probably just a residue, like Zab said. Happens sometimes with a longstanding spell. Wouldn't worry about it," he said, turning and heading toward the Sweet Shop.

That bastard. He'd done something else. Knew I shouldn't trust him.

21

I walked into the office where Zab, Musso, and Bibbi were already seated. Seemed all three of them were compulsively early, even as I'd tried to beat them all here. The idea of being first to work had settled my nerves about the new position.

Zab nodded. Musso gave me a halfhearted grunt.

Bibbi eyed up my outfit. "Very cute. I saw that on the mannequin and loved it."

I smoothed down the dark blue velvet of my fitted dress. It was something I never would've worn in Salem. It had a little too much *look at me* for what I typically would wear. But being a broker, they'd all be looking at me anyway, as if they weren't already. If they were all going to look at me, maybe it was time to own it? After all, I wasn't the girl who hid anymore.

Didn't hide, didn't hide, didn't hide. It was going to stick one of these times.

I walked to Belinda's...to my desk and ran a hand over the surface. There was already a pile of sorted slips sitting on it.

"You can sit at it too if you want," Musso said.

"Oh, there's a note for you too. Came this morning," Bibbi said, pointing to the folded sheet of memo paper.

Don't forget our cocoa date tonight.

Gregor

I had forgotten we were going for cocoa. But had I forgotten it was a date? Was that what I'd agreed to? I'd thought we were just friends. I slipped the note in the drawer.

"So what should I do?" I asked.

Zab walked over with a book and flipped it open, pointing to different lines. "Every transaction has to be logged into this book and then signed off here by the broker who negotiated the work." He pointed to a column and then another. "And then the agent who performed the work goes here."

"How do I know who to call for a job?"

"Musso and I will help you get going. You'll get to know your regulars after a while, and it gets easier. You start learning who's good in what situation and such." He shut the book and left it on my desk.

"And who's going to screw it all up," Musso added from his side of the room.

Hawk walked in from the back. His gaze ran the length of me. Hawk always seemed to know where I was in a room, but this time his eyes seemed to get stuck on me. And then mine got stuck on him because he wouldn't unstick his. This was why I didn't wear *look at me* clothes. Now he was looking at me. Worse, I *liked* it.

I walked into the back room and poured a cup of tea. It took me two minutes to own up to the fact that I'd run and hidden. Yes, I'd wanted tea, but the urge had come on suddenly, along with the running urge.

I don't run anymore. Except apparently I did.

Hawk followed me in a couple of minutes later.

I refused to leave this room until after he did. I was not going to run and hide again, even if I had to stand in the back room all day.

He walked over by the tea station I'd just departed, making himself something. He wasn't outright looking at me, and I wasn't staring at him point-blank, and yet it felt like we were still locked in a gaze. Something had to be done. It felt like boundaries were about to be crossed.

"Did you have something to do with the black cloud? It was suspiciously gone right after you hired me."

Now I wasn't hiding. I was fighting instead. Definite improvement. This was a man to have boundaries with, and I needed to keep us squarely on separate sides.

"No, I didn't. Don't you have a new job to do? I do believe we have a contract of employment, and I have to say, you don't appear to be working that hard." He turned, looking at me over his cup of coffee as he leaned on the table behind him. He leaned because he didn't run. That was what non-runners looked like.

"Just look me in the eyes and tell me you had nothing to do with the black cloud." I leaned against the couch, like a non-runner.

"I believe I already answered that."

Oscar walked in the back door. It was like the guy had an aversion to the front entrance.

"Heard there was a new broker in town," he said as he walked over and leaned on the other couch, giving me a once-, twice-, thrice-over. "You really upped your game for the new job, huh? Very nice indeed. So, what are you doing later on tonight? Want to go for a drink to celebrate your new position and maybe discover a couple other new positions while we're at it?" Oscar was smiling. How had I not realized what a playboy he was the first time I'd met him? Or the second time? It could've been tattooed on his forehead and not been any clearer than his come-hither smile and the twinkle in his eye that promised a good, long night, or a short, rough ride, depending on your preference. He was definitely looking to please as long as you didn't plan on overstaying your welcome.

And why was it that Oscar was eyeballing me and there was no desire to run and hide or beat him with my fists? All I wanted to do with him was laugh. Now why was that?

"She's not free," Hawk said, clearly telling Oscar to back off.

"Oh yeah, that's right. I heard you had plans with Gregor tonight. So the rumors are true? Didn't think he'd be your type for some reason."

I didn't know what rumors were circulating, but it was easy enough to guess. If Hawk wasn't standing there looking at me like he owned me, I might've elaborated on our situation or lack thereof. I could've told Oscar that Gregor was just a friend. But what fun would that be when Hawk was staring at me the way he was?

"Gregor is a nice guy. Why wouldn't he be my type?"

I focused all my attention on Oscar, refusing to look at Hawk, afraid I'd crumble and tell him it wasn't true. If

Hawk didn't approve of Gregor, all the more reason to go out with him.

Oscar shrugged. "I don't know. He seems *too* nice, like in a 'strip the fudge off a sundae' kind of way. I always pictured you as a 'rocky road, double caramel, loaded with whip, a handful of nuts and cherries' kind of gal. You know, no holds barred, no holding back, leave it all in the ring, no regrets, going at it until you're a puddle of sweat and your body collapses."

I should tell Oscar to shut up and mind his own business, but it was nearly impossible not to play along with him a little, especially as he was clearly having so much fun with it.

I leaned. "Really now? What would give you that idea?" I asked, jumping up to sit on the bookcase behind me, crossing my legs slowly, letting the hem ride up over the tall boots to show off a nice flash of thigh, like I was some seductress. I didn't even know where this was coming from. I'd never been flirty in my life.

Oscar smiled. "You play it close to the vest but you've got a mighty hot fire burning inside. I can feel the heat from across the room."

"Do you plan on dating Oscar now too? Why limit yourself to two? Why don't you date Zab as well, or Zark?" Hawk asked, nothing playful about his tone.

"Maybe I will," I replied.

"We'll see about that," he said. He smiled, as if he was daring me to try.

What the hell did that mean?

He grabbed his jacket and walked out.

Suddenly the game lost all of its amusement.

"He used to be a lot more fun. I don't know what happened to him," Oscar said, the twinkle in his eye flattened. He straightened up. "You do look good, though," he said, without a trace of flirtation left.

"Thanks," I replied, speaking to him like he was my brother. I wasn't sure what game Oscar and I were playing, but it seemed to have the same rules and end time. "Have to get to work."

He gave me a wink before he turned to make himself a coffee.

22

I walked along the perimeter of the wall I'd made, the one that might not last much longer, still in awe of what I'd done. How had I made such a thing when I couldn't do the simplest of spells?

I trailed my hand along the surface, feeling the mark of my magic all along it, finally understanding what they meant about tracking. The more familiar you became with magic, the more you picked up on its individual flavors. It could almost be compared to cooking or baking, and everyone had their own recipe. Some people liked a little more salt, some wanted to spice things up, but we all made the dish differently.

The other thing I picked up when I was here was hate. I couldn't seem to avoid it. There was something more going on here, and I couldn't deny it anymore.

"Why do you hate me? And I know it's not because of this," I said, running my hand along the wall. "You were trying to get rid of me as soon as I got here, but why? I know you can communicate. Just tell me why."

The crystal of the wall had a chill, but it wasn't ice. I

didn't think it was crystal, either. I wasn't sure what it truly was, and I'd made it. I walked farther along and shuddered. There was more heaviness leaking out, along with pure anger.

Another ten minutes of walking brought me to the newest crack, but someone had already beaten me to it. Hawk was running a hand over it. Should've guessed he already knew about it.

"Another new one," he said. His attention was on the fissure that ran ten feet vertically.

I stepped closer, hating the feel of the thing beyond the wall but needing a closer look.

He stepped back, giving me room and looking as if he wanted to hear what I had to say. It was the strangest feeling, how he always seemed to have more confidence in me than I had in myself.

And then he booted me. Don't forget that part. Don't ever forget.

I shrugged it off, trying to focus.

"If I could make this thing, I should be able to repair it. So why can't I?" I ran a hand up and down over the weak spot, knowing that the thing I'd contained was growing more dangerous and potent every day. "If this breaks completely, what will happen?"

Sometimes silence is comforting. This wasn't, not with the gravity of the moment. It was like standing at the edge of the abyss of nothingness, knowing that if you shouted out, nothing would shout back and there would be no echo. It would just disappear, and perhaps you would too.

I turned around, not saying a word. I didn't have to. My stare said it for me.

He stared back, and I didn't like the answer I saw there.

"I know it won't be good, but how bad?"

"I can't tell you what I don't know." He stepped closer, laying his hand near the fissure again. "I can only say what my gut is telling me, and it's almost never wrong."

Had his gut told him to get rid of me? If it had, I didn't like his gut. His gut was bullshit.

"If you don't mind, I need a little time alone here to feel out the situation," I said to him, the same way some people tell you to go screw.

"What are you thinking?" he asked, intent on my opinion.

The man was impervious to insult sometimes. Or was he too thick to realize I'd told him to leave?

"I don't know yet. That's why I was looking for some time alone."

"Most of the time, it's better to bounce ideas off other people."

"I don't want to bounce anything off you. I want you to leave."

He leaned a hand on the wall as he stared at me. "I understood that the first time you said it. Clearly I'm not leaving, so what were you thinking?"

"Why do you have to be so damned difficult? Why can't you go? I don't want to work with you all the time. It's bad enough I'm back living with you."

He leaned a shoulder against the wall, as if he were just standing in the forest having a relaxing moment while I lost my shit on him. It made me want to rage even more. "Everything has to be your way, and you don't care how anyone else feels or what they want. You, you, and you. That's all that matters."

He raised an eyebrow, silently asking if I were through.

I shrugged like I was having a spasm, finally spitting out, "What?"

He shook his head. "Did that make you feel better?"

"No."

"Then what do you need? Because there's work to be done, and we can't afford you to be emotional and causing problems. You're going to have to figure out a way to get along with me until we rectify this issue."

That was it. My emotions were an issue, because I had some. That must be a really big drag to him, with his shriveled-up black heart.

"What I need is for you to be human," I said, turning and walking away from him.

"You're going to be waiting a long time for that one," he said, remaining where he was.

I didn't know if he was being figurative or literal. Neither would surprise me.

23

I'll quit drinking the day after my fiftieth if I can just have one last good party.

I flipped through the directory of names in the book Zab had given me, skimming for parties. There were twenty different names. Seemed parties paid well, or they were quick, easy work.

"Who's the best person to call for a good birthday party? There are a lot of names. Is there a better or worse witch or warlock?" I asked, holding up the slip that had been in the pile on my desk. I looked at Zab, consciously ignoring the fact that Hawk had just walked into the office. Also trying to ignore the way Bibbi was watching Hawk enter the office, Oscar in tow.

"What kind of party? Any hint of what they consider a good party? Are they looking for raunchy or clean?" Zab asked, slumping back in his chair and kicking his feet up on his desk. Clearly he was unaware of all the tension that had just been lit inside this room.

"It's a fiftieth. No other mention. Just that they'll quit drinking after it."

Hawk was on the other side of the office still, talking to Oscar. He was leaning on the bookshelf, his arms crossed in front of him, showing off his good side, of which he had two.

When someone looked the way he did, it was hard not to glance over from time to time. It didn't mean anything. It was akin to looking at a pretty painting. Just because I admired the way something looked, didn't mean I wanted to marry the thing or have its babies. It only meant it looked good.

Hawk looked my way, and the heat in his eyes could have seized my engine. I turned toward Musso for a little cooldown. I couldn't overheat like this in public. People would get the wrong idea.

"Musso, what do you think?" I asked, turning so I could cut Hawk out of my peripheral vision.

"If they're a drinker, might mean they want a bit more than a good game of dominos. I'd newsflash Sadie P.," Musso said.

"I'll do it," Zab said, grabbing the newsflash papers before I could get them.

"It might not be a dragon every time," I said, keeping my back to Hawk and focusing on the job at hand.

"And it might be," Musso said.

"Hey, what happens if this person has a good party and then doesn't quit drinking?" I jotted Sadie P. down on the slip and added it to my job pile.

"Not good," Musso said.

Helen's gears spun long, slow, and loud, as if to second that remark.

I saw Oscar leaving out of the corner of my eye as

Hawk headed over. He stopped by my desk, picked up the slip, and looked at it.

"You can't put that kind of promise out into the universe and not uphold it. There will be payment one way or another, and it won't be good. Disease, possibly death." He dropped the slip back onto my desk.

I nodded, trying not to engage too much. I picked up one of my cheater books, as Zab had called them, and flipped through it for the average rates for parties. I was trying hard not to look at Hawk, who had decided to sit on my desk and flip though my slips.

He reached over, grabbed one of my books, and flipped through that next. I reread the same passage for the third time, trying to ignore his existence. It wasn't working well. Some people can scream right beside you and barely register. Some can whisper and you hear every word. Hawk was in the latter group.

"Talking about entertainment, how was yours last night?" Hawk asked, continuing to flip through the book.

"I don't think that's appropriate work conversation." This was definitely work, and he was most definitely not my friend.

"That doesn't sound very good. I'm not surprised you don't want to discuss it."

Great. I was now forced to either keep quiet and confirm his belief—which, unfortunately, was true—or elaborate and confirm his belief anyway.

I'd have to say nothing. I would rise above. I could do it. I'd fly like an eagle above the riff raff as I read the same passage for the fourth time.

"That bad, huh? I didn't want to tell you, but he did seem a bit dull."

"He's not dull. He's very interesting." And the regal

eagle was swooping down to catch some fish in the muddy swamp. So much for rising above.

"I'm sure he can talk about something. Did you discuss drink recipes? Did he try to hold your hand while you sipped cocoas? He doesn't seem the type to grab your hair and throw you up against the building."

Had he been watching us? Or was Gregor that predictably boring? I glanced around the office, wondering how many people were listening. Zab and Musso *seemed* to be working. Poor Bibbi had her hand on her chin, staring at Hawk with unadulterated lust.

"I have a lot of work to do, and I'm already very tired from my night out. And as I said, this isn't appropriate work conversation."

"Sure. You must be wiped out after getting in right after moonrise. How many hours of sleep could you even squeeze in? Ten? Eleven?"

I ignored him. There was nothing else that would help my case anyway. He was right. I didn't know when moonrise was, but I did know how early I'd gotten back, and apparently he did as well. He wasn't in the office when I'd come in, but he had something rigged to let him know who walked in this place at all times. I'd have to figure out a way around that.

He stood. I kept my eyes firmly on the papers in front of me.

Bibbi let out a sigh as Hawk left. She always did as he departed. She was too young to realize what she was getting into, even if she was my age. There was young on the calendar and then there was young and green. I'd never seen a pasture in spring after a good week of rain that could compete with how green this girl was. Hawk would chew her up, if he took more than a second to notice her.

I was going to have to have a talk with that girl. It was almost noon. Perfect timing.

"Bibbi, you want to go get cocoa with me?"

She glanced up, looking about as if she wasn't sure I was speaking to her.

"Do you want to go?" I said, walking to her desk.

"You mean you want me to go get you cocoa?" she asked.

Okay, I might not have thrown off the most welcoming vibes when I'd first met her, but had I been that bad? Maybe it was that magic caste system. Did she think I wouldn't want to go anywhere with a Whimsy?

"I'm asking if you want to go *with* me."

"Yes!" She shot out of her seat, knocking it over in her excitement. Then she knocked her basket over in the process of picking the chair up.

"Bibbi, go. I got it," Zab said, sweeping up all the slips.

"Okay," she said, scrambling to get her jacket.

"So how's it going? Do you like it at the broker's office?" I asked as we crossed the street.

"Oh, it's great."

"Do you like working for Hawk?"

Her smile dimmed a little, and she nodded.

"He isn't mean to you, is he?" I asked.

"No. Not at all."

"Then what is it?"

Her face turned bright red. "I wish he'd look at me the way he looks at you," she said.

Since I was the only one here, she had to be speaking to me. Still, I glanced around to make sure. Nope, just the two of us. Shit. Now I had to say something back.

"He doesn't look at me that..." That sounded like a bald-faced lie, considering the way Hawk had just looked at me. This was really not the way I'd planned on starting this conversation. "He's not the type of man you should *want* to look at you like that. He's not someone you can have a real relationship with."

She nodded. At least she wasn't utterly delusional about the situation.

She paused outside the shop. "Just so you know, I didn't always like him. He was damn near mean when I first started working here. Barely tolerable. When he hired me, he said in passing that it was driving him crazy that no one was sitting at that table. Then, my first day, he kept looking at my table and nearly growled at me. If he didn't pay well, I would've quit that day. He was scary and moody and just unlikeable. He was pretty much what everyone said he was, but he wasn't in that much, and, like I said, the pay was good."

"Then what happened?" I was shaking my head.

"One day he came in and wasn't so scary anymore. He seemed happier. He was joking with Musso and Zab a lot and seemed like a different person. You wouldn't under-stand because you showed up a week or so after he stopped being so angry." Her eyebrows scrunched together. "Wait, you did know him before, though, right? Was he like that when you met him too? Is that why you're still mad at him?"

She kept staring at me, waiting for an answer.

"Yeah, no, he was like that with me too." Had he really been different after I was gone? It made no sense, consid-ering he'd forced me out. Then when I finally got back, he'd tried to force me out again. Maybe he was happy because he needed help with the wall? There was no way he was happy I was back, not when he was trying to force me out.

24

The broker house was closed for the night, and Gregor would show up any second. Hopefully he'd be the only one. Now that it was empty, the coast was clear. I took a look in the mirror, shifted the dress, fixed the laces on my boots, and gave my hair a fluff.

I shot downstairs to grab a quick tea, but there was other business to handle first. Helen's gears churned as soon as I stepped inside the office. It was the perfect opportunity.

"Helen, do you know why I got the black cloud?"

Her gears stopped churning. Well, that was a "no" if I'd ever heard one. Helen knew a lot but apparently didn't want to share this tidbit. Maybe there were rules about what she could share?

"Fine. You can't or won't say. Maybe you're friends with whoever doles out the black clouds. Can you tell me who put Braid and Spike up to picking me up in Salem?"

Still silence.

"Are you giving me the silent treatment?" Why wasn't Helen talking to me?

The door opened behind me and Hawk walked in.

He leaned a hip on the counter as his eyes took in the extra fluff of my hair and then seemed to get stuck at my glossed lips.

"Waiting for Gregor?" He raised a brow.

"Yes." He already knew Gregor was coming, so no use in denying it. I wouldn't clarify our relationship, either. I didn't ask him where he was most of the time. He didn't have a right to know my every move.

"I don't like him," he said.

"I do." I crossed my arms, trying to stare him down, knowing it was nearly impossible. He didn't run from conflict. He wasn't made that way.

"What is it that you want from me?" I asked. "You force me out and then force me back here. You make it impossible to get a job and then give me one. Now you want to dictate who I see? What do you want? Just tell me."

He walked over to me, and before I had the chance to argue anymore, his hands were on my waist, hoisting me to the shelf that brought me eye level with him.

His lips were on mine as his hands moved to my hips, tugging me closer to him, his cock coming flush against my core as he stepped in between my legs.

His air became mine as he flexed his hips just enough to cause another gasp from my lips as my head fell back. This, right here, was what I'd feared. The second he touched me, all logic disappeared. All I could think of was the brush of his lips against the flesh of my neck.

I didn't push him away. I clung to him as if we were longtime lovers. I burned inside as if he were meant for me, and only me.

When he pulled away, I gripped the wood I was sitting on to not yank him back to me.

I hopped off the shelf, expecting to see that same annoyed expression.

He was smiling.

"What do—"

Gregor was at the front door, knocking.

Hawk looked at the door. "Are you going to invite your date in?"

I narrowed my eyes at him, holding back what I wanted to say.

Gregor walked in and darted a look at Hawk and then back to me. "Everything okay?" he asked.

As much as I wished there was a little more heat or spine in him when he looked at Hawk, how could there be? Hawk wasn't normal. I couldn't judge Gregor for not being a lunatic, could I?

Hawk glanced at Gregor like he was looking at a bug he was too lazy to step on.

Hawk turned back to me. "Yes, Tippi, is everything okay? Is there a problem?"

I moved toward Gregor. "Everything is great. There's no problem here."

"Be ready at five tomorrow," Hawk said. "We have things to do."

Gregor reached out to me, touching my side. Hawk's gaze went right to it, and now the heat was there in spades.

I walked fast enough that Gregor's hand lost its perch as I made my way outside. The last thing I wanted was Gregor's blood on my hands.

"Sorry. This should only take a second, but if I don't do it, there'll be hell to pay," I said as Gregor and I walked back into the empty broker's office. As much as I didn't want any chance of dealing with Hawk again, if Dusty didn't get her second cocoa of the day, we'd all pay for it tomorrow. "Dusty, I've got your cocoa," I said.

Suddenly, a few feet away, a little light grey bunny hopped over.

Taking the lid off, I placed the cup on the ground as Gregor watched on. The bunny hopped over, and its nose grazed my hand before its little tongue darted out and licked me. I gave her a few pets on the head and said, "I'll be back in a little bit."

I straightened. "Okay, we can go now." The sooner I got Gregor out of the office, the better. If it wasn't for Dusty, I wouldn't have brought him back at all.

"Is that dust bunny your pet or something?" Gregor asked as we left the office.

"No. I just feed her cocoa. I occasionally pet her." I might find her in my bed occasionally, sleeping on top of me. "She might be."

"That's cool. You know, interesting."

Gregor brushed his hand against mine as we walked away from the broker's office for the second time, trying to see if I'd bite. I switched my cocoa to that side.

"Are you okay? I know you said everything was good, but it didn't look that way back in the office. You looked out of sorts."

His eyes were soft, and his voice filled with concern. He was sensitive, caring, and everything Hawk wasn't. He was *good*. If there wasn't a spark, there could be eventually. I needed to train myself to like the right boys, not the man who people crossed the road for.

"Yeah, I'm fine. It's just hard to work with him some-times. He doesn't always respect boundaries."

"In what way?" His voice grew an edge under all that softness.

"Oh, no, not like that." Was I an idiot? How could I even say something like that to him? Gregor wouldn't fare well against Hawk. He was too nice. You had to be a certain type of hard to have a chance against Hawk, and Gregor's slight edge wouldn't cut it.

"Then how? You can talk to me. You can trust me, Tippi. I would never hurt you."

The first night I ever came to the broker house, I'd asked Hawk if I could trust him. He'd implied it wouldn't matter what he said. It would mean nothing. He'd almost had me believing his crazy ways.

"He just has a belief in the way certain things should be that doesn't always line up. He gets frustrated."

Actually, plain old mad, and the list seemed to go on and on. He was mad I was in Xest. Mad I was going to get a job. Mad I couldn't protect myself, even though I was working on that.

"Tippi, talk to me. I won't judge you," Gregor said.

The streets were quiet tonight, but even as the sneerers occasionally passed, Gregor never seemed fazed, not even when the black cloud chased everyone else away.

"I know you're not judging me. I'm judging myself."

"You don't need to tell me. It's all right." He tucked his hands in his pockets as he looked ahead, strolling beside me.

We walked in easy silence for a little while, sipping our drinks. Maybe this was how it was supposed to be with the man you ended up with? Easy. Comfortable. I felt like I could tell him anything right now.

"I don't always measure up. For instance, I'm a protectorate who can't protect herself very well," I said.

"How is that possible? You fought off grouslies and a dragon," he said, as if I'd made up the most unbelievable tale.

"The grouslies left on their own. With the dragon, Zab was there. I'd probably be a piece of charcoal right now if it had been only me. I tend to do better when there are others who need help."

He shrugged, but he was grinning. "I don't think that's a problem. It's just you. You're a caring person. It makes sense you'd be tougher when protecting others."

He really didn't care. There was zero judgment.

"Hawk thinks it's a problem."

"Hawk is a bit extreme." He waved me along. "Come on, I want to show you something."

We walked to the edge of town and kept going until we were in a pasture with one of those large trees with black leaves and a grey trunk. All around it, tiny streams of blue light weaved their way toward the tree.

"What is this? It's beautiful."

He tilted his head toward me. "Streamers. Once a year, they come to this tree to mate." I took a step closer, but he held up a hand in front of me. "You can't get too close or they'll bite. They'll come after you in a swarm, and you'll be covered with red welts for a week."

"Good to know." I took a step back, and then another. "It's getting late. We should probably head back. I've got work in the morning."

"Heard about that. You're a pretty important person now, huh?"

"No. Just plain old Tippi."

"Nothing about you is plain," he said. He took my hand, and this time there wasn't any hesitation.

I stared down at his grip as he tugged me forward. I let

myself be pulled closer, knowing where this was heading even as I was unsure about the destination.

Gregor seemed like a fairly safe bet as far as men went. He didn't judge when I said I couldn't protect myself, and he wasn't walking and talking testosterone. If I got involved with him, I wouldn't be holding on for dear life at every turn. He was everything Hawk wasn't. He was everything I should want. As he bent his head down, I didn't turn away. Soft lips brushed tentatively over mine.

It wasn't bad even if there was a lack of something— urgency, passion, heat. Maybe it needed a little help? I lifted onto my tiptoes, wrapping my arms around his neck, trying to coax some heat into the moment.

He wrapped his arms around my back, arching me into him as he tried to delve with his tongue. Unfortunately, it hit the roadblock of my lips. Not one part of me wanted any part of him inside me, not even a portion of a tongue.

I pressed my hands on his shoulders, pushing out of his embrace. His lips stilled before he dropped his hands, his eyes crinkling at the corners and an unspoken question hanging on his parted lips.

"I'm sorry. I thought I was ready for something, but I don't think I am." Or not ready for *him*, and I wasn't sure I ever would be. There was a certain spark that was either there or it wasn't. This sparkler felt like it had been left out in the rain for a week, but he didn't need to know that. When Hawk touched me, I melted into him.

"Because of all the things going on?" Gregor asked, perfectly willing to accept that it wasn't him, even when it was.

"It's just a lot. I can't really get my head in order right now. You understand?"

"Of course. If you need some more time, I'm willing to wait."

He'd be waiting a long time, but I didn't have the heart to tell him that right now. There was a thread of truth; I had too much on my plate right now. I'd feel like that no matter who was standing in front of me, unless it was Hawk.

That didn't make Hawk the right man. It merely proved I was a touch crazy.

25

When Bautere crouched low, getting ready, there was no part of him that appeared to be playing. This didn't feel like a game or a sparring session. His growl filled the area, and when he charged for me, my heart beat like I was on the verge of death.

I leapt fifteen feet, rolled in the air, and landed behind him. It would've been amazing if it weren't half of what I'd tried to accomplish.

He turned, growling his displeasure. "You aren't attacking. As a protectorate, it's not instinctual to be aggressive, but you need to learn. Now again. This time, you attack."

I stretched my arms out, trying to psych myself up to purposely engage what appeared to be a massive polar bear. I took off, leapt into the air right before we would've collided, and tried to land a blow. It was as if all the gas in my tank had run out. I crashed to the ground on my left side, rolling a little too late to disperse the blow.

I didn't groan. I'd learned early that you suffered in silence unless you just couldn't hold it back. Any signal of weakness would simply alert your opponent where to aim.

"You need to find a way."

"I know," I said, getting to my feet, trying to ignore the pain.

He took in the way I was favoring my left leg. "We're done for the day." He walked off.

I got into the office an hour late for work. Zab, Musso, and Bibbi watched as I hobbled across the room.

"I tripped," I said, shutting down any questions as I settled at my desk, looking at the slips piling up.

I wasn't sure what was distracting me more: the pain in my knee or Bibbi staring at the door again, waiting for Hawk. Many people walked in and out of the office, but he was the only one she waited for. So much for our conversation yesterday.

Any second Hawk would walk in and pass by her, without so much as a nod. She'd get up and follow him, asking ten different questions that he would try to palm off on Musso or Zab. Did he not realize what was going on? When had I gone from resenting her neediness to wanting to build up her self-esteem enough that she wouldn't wait for any crumb? Probably right about the time this became too painful to witness.

As predicted, Hawk walked in and Bibbi stared hard. Hawk might've gestured in her direction, but it was such a slight movement that it was hard to discern whether it was an actual nod.

To make it worse, the monkeys kicked into "Reunited" by Peaches and Herb. Just what we needed to make the moment more awkward. I was about to drag a finger across my throat, signaling for them to cut it out, but I stopped. They were getting pretty good, and I hadn't heard this song in ages. Plus, Hawk had already walked into the back room.

Bibbi leaned forward, chin on her hand and eyes downcast. It was too much. Would it really kill him to say hello?

I stood, wincing at the pain as I walked into the back room, finding a perch on the edge of the couch.

"We need to talk," I said.

He was over at the cocoa/tea station, his back to me. He turned, his brows dropping and his face instantly intent. "Is there a problem?"

Considering I never sought him out, it was understandable that he might be alarmed, especially with everything happening.

"Not a problem, exactly," I said, shaking my head. I pointed to the office. "Can you mute the room?"

The din from the people talking in the office went away completely.

"So what did you want to speak to me about?" He tilted his head slightly, a spark in his eyes that made my breathing hitch.

Great. Now he thought this was about the kiss.

He leaned a shoulder on the bookcase beside him, crossed an ankle, and waited, looking too good for words. Why did he have to be attractive, even as I was annoyed with him? Clearly there was something wrong with me. But I wasn't the issue right now. Bibbi was. I wouldn't let him walk all over her the way he had with me and Belinda.

Oh no. Now I was grouping myself with Belinda. I needed to get to the point and end this conversation.

"I think Bibbi might have a crush on you."

He let out a soft laugh. "Your powers of observation are astounding. What tipped you off?"

I rolled my eyes. "Okay, so it's *obvious* she has a crush on you. Would it kill you to give her a little attention?"

"You want me to lead Bibbi on?" He raised his brows and crossed his arms.

"I'm not saying sleep with her. Just don't act like she's invisible." Sleeping with her would be a horrible idea. He'd destroy her. Definitely did not want that. "I'm not even telling you to kiss her. Just show her some attention."

He pushed off the shelf and walked closer. "And if she gets worse?"

"She won't." Now I doubted *his* powers of observation. She couldn't get any worse. But maybe it would build up her ego a little.

"It's not a good idea."

He shook his head as he leaned on the couch next to me, close enough that I could smell his woodsy scent.

"I think there might be an in-between area, don't you? Where maybe you give her some attention but not enough to lead her on?"

He leaned closer. "Not who I am. I'm either interested or not."

Oh, I was definitely not taking the bait on that one. As far as I was concerned, that kiss we'd had the other day had not happened.

"I'll owe you one." I moved a hair away, afraid if I didn't, I'd move closer.

"You'll owe me?" he asked, his smirk shooting my heart with adrenaline.

"Yes. Nothing crazy. Something of equal value."

His smirk turned into a confident smile. "Fine. I'll pay her more attention, but you owe me."

When had everything turned into a sexual innuendo? Was he doing it, or was I going there alone?

"Agreed," I said.

There was a snapping sound and a flash in the air. Shit. I'd made a contract. I had to get out of here before I walked into something else.

I got up from the couch and staggered a bit, forgetting to baby my left knee. Of course I'd nearly fall down in front of him to top off the day.

He stepped closer, looking at my knee. "What's wrong with your leg?"

"Nothing. I tripped." I went to move past him and back into the office. Out of sight, out of mind, even if it was just a room over.

He shifted, blocking me. "I didn't buy the door story, and I definitely don't buy that you tripped. Tell me what happened to your knee."

I shifted to the left.

He shifted with me. "I'm not asking again."

I rolled my eyes dramatically before meeting his gaze. "Oh, good. I thought you were going to keep at it all day."

Hawk went completely still. His eyes narrowed right before he looped an arm around my waist, hoisting me off the ground, walking us both over to the couch.

"Get off me," I yelled.

He tossed me on my back on the couch. Before I got my bearings, he tore the leg of my pants from the ankle up to my knee.

"What are you doing? These were my favorite pants!"

This wasn't like Salem. Did he have any idea what good clothes in Xest cost when they were all handmade?

I punched him in the arm. It didn't faze him.

"You're buying me a new pair."

He nailed me with a look that would've made a sane person lean back. I leaned forward, or tried to, but he put a hand on my stomach when I tried to get up.

Worst part was the way my body reacted to his touch. I leaned back just so I didn't encourage any more touching. Every tiny contact was like trying to extinguish a raging fire with gasoline.

"How did this happen to your knee?" he asked. "Who did this?"

"None of your business."

"You're walking around battered and refusing to tell me what the hell is happening?"

The veins in his neck were bulging, and I could feel the sizzle of his magic in the room, raising the temperature a few degrees.

"I'm not battered," I said, trying to pull the scraps of my pants over my knee.

He stood and called into the other room, "Zab?"

"Yeah?" Zab hesitantly called back.

"Close up for the day. Now."

There was a long pause before he replied, "Got it."

"What's the purpose of closing the shop? What's that going to do? I'm still not talking to you," I said, grabbing the throw blanket from the arm of the couch and draping it over my leg so he'd stop staring at it.

"You'll tell me eventually because you're not leaving here until you do." He sat on the opposite couch, stretched an arm across the back, and dared me to try to leave with his gaze.

It was a dare I had no problem taking. I never should've tried to talk to him. That was what I got for butting in to Bibbi's business.

I got up, hobbling for a second in spite of my best efforts, and went to leave the room. Let him try to keep me here. Right before I got to the door, it disappeared, becoming a cinder-block wall. I turned around and made a pitiful excuse for a dash for the back door, which was also now a cinder-block wall, along with the window.

"Let me out of here, now." I spun around to face him.

He leaned back. "No."

"You can't keep me here."

"Pretty sure I can."

I gave him my back, not knowing what to say. He might be right. He probably *could* keep me here, and what could I do to stop him? I wasn't totally useless, though. I just needed to figure out how to use my magic to get me out of this mess.

I thought back to the different spells I'd been memorizing at Zab's. Most of them were charms and notions. Nothing that would get me out of here. I was better off trying to help this room somehow. After all, that was what my magic liked to do.

"This room needs air," I said with a flick of my wrist.

A gust of wind from nowhere blew in. The cinder blocks didn't budge.

"This room needs ventilation." A ceiling fan appeared overhead.

"You're not getting out until I let you out," he said calmly. "This is my building. Nothing you do will offset what I put in place, not with the way I've warded it."

Of course it wouldn't. Still, there were other angles to work. As if he'd sit here all day. He'd crack. I'd never seen this man sit still since I'd known him, let alone what we were doing now. Just had to be patient. I had a decent amount of patience. I could get through this.

I walked over to the other couch and sat, leaning back the way he was. "Fine. Then we sit and wait."

An hour in and I was already second-guessing my vow to wait him out. Why wasn't I telling him? Oh, yeah, I was making a point. At least he was miserable too. I could tell by the way he was getting up for yet another cup of coffee.

"I could force you to tell me," he said, displaying the second chink in his armor, a weakness I'd suspected but was now sure of.

Oh, he was cracking.

"Why does it matter? It's my knee."

"You work in my office, sleep in my building—that makes you untouchable. If I have to interrogate every single person that lives in Xest to find out how these accidents are happening, I will."

Suddenly my armor had a chink as well. An image of him going building to building, questioning everyone as if I couldn't take care of myself? It was too much. They'd think I was weak. It would set my reputation back for a decade. Right now, I was the Nowhere witch. What would I be after that? I hadn't thought there was something worse than Whimsy witch, and I'd been wrong then. Would he really take it that far? The two of us had crossed many lines, but this one was different. This could destroy my reputation.

"You'd make people think I can't take care of myself?"

With a glance at my knee, he said, "Clearly you can't."

"Nobody did this to me, or no one around here."

"Then who?"

"Tell me why you deserve to know anything that happens with me. Answer that and I'll answer you."

"Because whether you believe it or not, I give a fuck if you're getting hurt."

Damn this man. The way he said it, the heat in his eyes, it was hard not to believe him. There was also the problem that it was very possible he would go to every person in Xest. He'd won—again—and, if possible, I was even angrier about this than everything else, because it came down to the same problem I always had with him.

"I'm getting hurt practicing how to protect myself. There you go. There's the sordid truth. Are you happy? It's not a marauding gang of haters. That's all you're going to get, and it's more than you deserve."

"Why didn't you come to me for help?"

"Because I didn't want to. You don't help. You force me into doing what you think is best. You don't consider what I want, what I think is best for me. Why *would* I come to you?"

I got up and walked to the door, shaking by the time I got there.

"You've got your answer, now let me out," I said, pounding a fist on the cinder blocks. Then the wall was gone. I didn't know if he'd done it or if I'd managed, but I wasn't going to stick around long enough to ask.

26

Gregor walked into the office with two cocoas. The looks he got from everyone there, you would've thought he was in a clown outfit.

He nodded to the rest of the room as he made his way to my desk. "I was in the area, so I figured you might want a cocoa. I brought a second for..." He glanced around, looking at the floor.

"Dusty?" He'd brought the dust bunny cocoa? Okay, the kiss hadn't been good. Still, how did you toss someone who'd bring your pet cocoa?

"Yeah." He placed both cups in front of me. "You around later?" he asked quietly, his eyes shooting around to the audience we had.

Even the monkeys were watching. It was like these savages never saw someone get asked on a date before.

Zab shot me a look, as if I needed a reminder that I had to practice wards tonight. All I thought about were charms, wards, notions, defense, and references.

"I've got some things I need to do with Zab, but maybe tomorrow?"

"Sounds good," Gregor said. Zab, Musso, and Bibbi tried not to stare at him as he left, but they didn't do a great job of it.

Bibbi was chewing on the end of her pencil, staring at me.

"So, you think that's what I should be shooting for?" she asked. "Like, that's a good pick?"

Zab made a snoring noise. Musso grunted. The monkeys started playing "Rock-a-bye Baby."

Hawk strode into the office.

Bibbi shook her head. "I don't think I'm strong enough," she said to me.

Hawk walked over toward me, stopping at Bibbi's table.

"You look very pretty today, Bibbi," he said, smiling at her.

Then he turned to me with a look that said, *Satisfied?*

Actually, no. He wasn't supposed to tell her she was pretty. He was only supposed to acknowledge her. If he took it too far, she'd end up more into him. Unless he really thought she looked pretty. He never said that to me, no matter how cute I dressed.

"We've got an appointment," he said, narrowing his eyes at the two cocoas on the desk.

"For what? I've got a lot of appointments set up for today." I took the lid off the second cocoa, put it on the floor, and made a clucking noise.

"Zab and Musso will have to cover them. It's something for the wall." He was watching as I put the cocoa on the floor, as if it was a key to some mystery.

"I thought we were partners. You're supposed to confer with me, not dictate." I was already standing and piling up my slips to give to Zab.

"An opportunity arose that I had to take. If you don't want to come, I'll handle it alone." Hawk headed out the door.

"Oh no. You're not going without me." I grabbed my jacket, running after him.

He was already halfway down the block when I caught up to him.

"Where are we going? Who are we meeting?"

"It's a connection of Mertie's who can supply us with something to help repair the wall."

"Mertie? The demon from the factory? What kind of connections does she have?" Mertie and I hadn't really hit it off. Who knew what she might've repeated to her connection? Hopefully it wasn't much, or we wouldn't be getting anything.

"Where's the appointment?" I asked.

"It's difficult to describe. You'd be hard-pressed to find it on a map," he said, seeming a hair more intent than normal.

"Hey, Tippi," one of the customers I knew from Zark's said as he passed us on the other side of the street. His smile faded and a more dignified and resigned expression came over him as he said, "Hawk."

"Hey, Buzzy." I waved. Did I have him on my list? I didn't think I'd written his name down. He might be willing to stand up as a reference for me on immigration day.

"How do you know Buzzy?" Hawk asked.

Hawk was probably annoyed I might be developing friendships in Xest because all the people should belong to him.

"Zark's. Is that a problem?" I asked.

"No. Is it an issue that I ask?" he said, mocking my tone.

"Why would it be?"

We took a couple more steps in silence before I saw another familiar face.

"Felix, hope you're not hitting the hills too hard," I said as a man with waist-length hair came by, his best friend beside him. "Helix, you keep him under control."

"You know I can't," Helix said as the two passed. "When you coming back to Zark's?"

"Not sure, but I'll let you know."

I definitely didn't have them on my list. That was three people I could add to my reference list.

Hawk had stopped walking, and I pulled the little notebook out of my pocket, jotting their names down. If I could get them, that would put me at twenty-six.

"Keeping a count of all the people you know for some reason?" Hawk asked, glancing over my shoulder.

"It helps me remember names," I said, smiling even when we both knew I was lying.

He hadn't said a word to me about immigration, but there was no way he *didn't* know. He had too many spies in Xest. For all I knew, the monkeys might've told him. They were about as loyal as a pet snake, and that might be giving the snake a bad name.

I tucked my notepad back in my pocket.

He grabbed my hand. I stared at the connection, knowing it wasn't romantic. Gregor was a hand holder. Hawk was more likely to grab you by the back of the head.

"I'll have to help you in," he said. "We have to wait here for a few minutes, though."

I looked about the square. "You said we couldn't find the place on a map. Where exactly is this appointment?"

"The entrance will be here soon. He's expecting us."

I wish I'd stopped for a cocoa for this walk, especially if there was going to be a lot of standing around and holding hands. It would give me something else to pretend to be distracted by.

A cloud floated in front of the sun, casting us in a harsh shadow.

"Come on," Hawk said, tugging at me. He didn't let go as he walked right beside me down the street.

The sun seemed to dim more, and the blue skies turned dark grey. The people who were walking the streets began to look fuzzy, and then they disappeared completely.

Other ones appeared, except these people I'd never seen before, and it was getting so that I recognized most of the faces in Xest. There was something weird about these people, too. They walked as if they had no destination, their pace oh so slow but steady. No one nodded or sneered as they glanced our way.

"What's going on? Where are we?"

All I got was a tip of his head and a shrug of his shoulder. "You can't figure it out?"

I looked around at the place that still resembled Xest but wasn't quite Xest.

"Are we in hell?" I whispered. "Did you take me to hell and not tell me? And you wonder why I think you're a horrible person."

"It's not hell. Next level up," he said, smiling, because only Hawk would be amused in purgatory.

"I'll never look at these streets the same."

"It's not just Xest. This place is everywhere, even Salem. It's simply a different dimension." He looked at me as if he was surprised I hadn't figured that out.

Growing up, there were certain things I thought I'd want to know if given the chance, like heaven and hell, UFOs and aliens. This was something I could've done without knowing.

"What if they try to keep one of us? I mean, I'm not pointing fingers or anything, but is this safe?"

The lunatic laughed. "There's a pact in place for these types of events. Can't keep up unless we die naturally. And not sure they'd want me anyway, but thank you for the concern."

"What if this pact doesn't pertain to me because I'm not from Xest?"

"Just don't let go of my hand," he said.

Seriously? I was a handhold away from possibly getting stuck here? I clenched his hand tight enough that I might've broken a finger or two.

"You think maybe you could've added some of these details when I asked where the appointment was?"

"Would you have come?" he asked.

"G—" Probably not the time to use his name and draw attention to myself. "Definitely not."

"Then it's good I didn't tell you. The person we have an appointment with wanted to meet you, and they might have something that will work on the wall."

"I'm so not happy with you right now."

"It's purgatory. You'll blend better."

A man with slicked-back hair and eyes that glowed red appeared in the distance. He was sitting at a desk made of slabs of rough stone in a place that I would've called the square on a normal day.

"Is that..." Keeping a firm hold of Hawk's hand, I tugged him in the other direction.

"That's not him. He's booked a decade out."

Okay, so not the devil—only a lower-level cleric, maybe? He probably couldn't hijack me to hell. Hawk tugged me forward with him, and I fell into step.

"Hawk, I presume?"

Hawk nodded.

The cleric gave him a once-over before turning his attention to me, where it lingered much longer. "And the witch," he said, putting his elbow on his desk, his fingers forming a steeple. He smiled wide enough to show off black, pointy fangs.

My fingers dug into Hawk's hand.

"Do you have it?" Hawk asked.

The cleric reached down, lifted a metal bucket, and placed it on top of his desk. "It'll refill as needed."

Hawk stepped forward and took the pail.

"There'll be a debt," the cleric said, smiling my way again.

"The introduction already paid for that," Hawk said, stepping in front of me.

"Had to try." The cleric shrugged and then leaned around Hawk to look at me in a way that made my stomach turn. "You are definitely on our radar, *witch*."

There was a strange intonation to the way he said witch, as if he were implying I might be something else.

"Is there anything you'd like to share?" Hawk asked the cleric, never one to let an implication die quietly.

"Nothing at all. Absolutely nothing. We'll be watching. We have a vested interest in how this works out. Whatever this thing is, we can't have it leaking over into our dimension, so we'll expect you to handle it. Otherwise, we might be forced to get involved."

"Stick to your own territory. I'm handling it," Hawk said.

The cleric looked at me again. "It was very nice to meet you, Tippi. I'm sure you'll be offering plenty of entertainment for us."

We walked back in the direction we'd come, but I didn't speak or unclench his hand until the sun was shining again.

"Don't ever take me there again. Why did he even want to meet me? Guess you didn't feel that was important to tell me either?"

"I didn't know. That's why I brought you. I was trying to find out."

I pointed to the bucket. "What is that stuff?"

"They use it to reinforce the boundaries between their dimensions and keep certain undesirables locked away. We're going to see if it works on your wall."

27

"Why am I doing this alone?" I asked, as I smeared the black, tar-like substance over the fissures in the wall. Every handful felt like it had tiny worms squirming around in it, and no matter how much I used, it kept replenishing. Logically, that was a good thing, and I reminded myself of that every scoop.

"It's your wall. It'll adhere better if applied by you." Hawk leaned on the wall beside me as he watched. "Saw Gregor leaving the office today."

I glanced around, knowing I couldn't up and leave. I was held hostage by black goop from another dimension, and this conversation wasn't going anywhere good. He'd probably start prying about how things were going with Gregor. Then I'd feel compelled to make something up just to not prove him right. I grabbed a big handful of goop, slopping it on as if I were too preoccupied by my work to talk.

"I'm surprised you're letting this continue," he said, as if amusing himself. "You like a little sizzle. Gregor doesn't sizzle. He's like flat marsh water that smells a little rotten."

"And let me guess, you're all bubbly?" I splattered half the black goop on the ground. Shit.

"I was talking about Gregor."

He was smirking. He knew damned well he sizzled. His ego nearly floated on all his fizzy bubbles, and I wouldn't help inflate it anymore.

I stopped mid-scoop to look him in the eye. "Well, you don't. You're like seltzer that's lost all its bubbles but still thinks it's got something over plain old well water."

He stopped staring but was still smiling, as if even my insults amused him. I wasn't confident enough to believe he'd given up on riling me up, but I'd let the silence hang, pretending for a few moments that the conversation was done as I tried to repair the last break.

I'd placed my other hand on the wall, trying to use both hands to press the goop in as deep as I could, when a strange feeling seeped through. I moved my hands around the area, trying to find the source.

"You picking up on something?" Hawk asked, moving close enough that his shoulder was brushing mine. At least this was about business.

"I'm picking up something weird, but I don't understand it." I ran my fingers over different areas until I nailed down the strongest spot, which seemed to be where the break had started. "Or why I've never felt it before. Maybe it's this stuff that's letting me sense it now?"

I'd been working on this crack longer than any of the rest, and it was the worst one of all.

Hawk moved his hand around to different places, looking more impatient with each second. "Explain it to me," he said, when he couldn't seem to find a spot to feel it himself.

"I don't know how. It's just this sense that something is

off, but I can't figure out why or how I know it. When I touch it, it's almost like a feeling of being spun in a circle a bunch of times."

He laid his hand over mine where it was pressed against the wall.

"What are you doing?" I asked.

"I'm trying to feel what you're feeling." He pressed harder against my hand.

"Can you feel it?"

"No. You've got me locked out so tight I'm getting nothing. You need to let me in."

I ignored his sizzle, the one I'd insisted he didn't have, and tried to keep my focus on the wall, on the feeling, so that maybe he could pick up on it somehow.

His other arm came up on my other side, so he was nearly embracing me as he laid that hand on top of my other, his heat seeping along the length of me.

"You need to try harder," he said.

"I am."

"If you don't concentrate and let me in a little, we'll be here all day," he said, with a little more huskiness in his voice.

How was I possibly going to let him in when my entire day, from dawn to dusk, was focused on keeping him out? I'd made blocking Hawk a part-time job, and I'd been at it for months.

But did I want this wall fixed or not? Did I want to let the wall slowly crumble until this evil took over Xest? At least with this, we were on the same page. He wanted it as much as I did.

"How do I let you in?" I asked, never imagining I'd say those words, as his skin sizzled where it touched me.

"Feel my magic pulsing against you? Just let it move

into you." His jaw grazed my ear, sending little tingles through me.

Let him in. Let his pulsing energy in. Why did that not seem like a good idea on any level? Because it wasn't for me. As far as the wall went, it was a no-brainer. I tried to let down my defenses, which meant not thinking at all. If I thought about purposely letting him in, I'd do the opposite. Even now, my body was going rigid.

He let go on one of my hands and cupped my face, turning it toward him.

"Don't think. Just relax," he said.

He leaned down, the scruff of his shadowed jaw grazing my cheek, and all I could smell was his woodsy scent. The fifth wind stopped as his heat enveloped me. His lips grazed mine, teasing until I closed the rest of the distance.

The purpose of the kiss was clear. This was business. It didn't change the heat that boiled up in me, or the feelings that it dredged up with it, the need that always overcame me with his touch.

I molded into him, and we fit together seamlessly. He was throwing off massive amounts of heat that seemed to seep into me, making it even easier to relax into him, let him take whatever he wanted.

No, no, no. You don't let him take whatever he wants.

I pulled back, scared by how fast I'd fallen again.

If he knew how startled I was, he didn't show it. He was looking at the wall.

"The magic is missing something. It was there, but it's being leached away in spots. That's what's causing the breaks."

"Why? How?"

He shook his head. "I don't know, but hopefully the patch will work."

"Did you feel anything else?" I asked.

"Like what?"

I stared at the wall, knowing I sensed a hatred seething out behind it, directed at me. "I don't know. Nothing, I guess."

I shifted away, instantly missing Hawk's heat as I did. He didn't try to stop me and let me have my space.

I grabbed another handful of goop, trying to make quick work of the last of this. I needed to get away from him, and fast. I'd get my head back together in private.

He leaned on the wall beside me again. "By the way, I thought I was flat, no sizzle?"

Clearly, he'd felt more than just the wall when I'd let him in.

"Like day-old seltzer," I said, continuing to work even as my cheeks burned.

He crossed his arms, getting more comfortable. "I'm not sure why you keep trying to make things work with Gregor."

"I'm not surprised you'd think that, considering the way your relationships work out."

"My relationships?" He raised a brow.

"Belinda? That was a grand success?"

He laughed. Hawk's laughing was almost as addictive as his kissing. It made my stomach swirl in the craziest ways. I'd have to make a point of trying not to amuse him, not that I'd meant to.

"I'm glad you find the mockery of your situation so funny."

I tried to highlight the fact I was insulting him, and he smiled wider. Not good.

"You should probably break it off now if you care about him," he said. "It's cruel to string him along, since it's not going to work out."

"You have no idea whether my relationship with him will work out, so I suggest you mind your own business." Half my goop was landing on the ground at this point, and I didn't care. I needed to be done.

He gave a slight shrug. "I've got a pretty good idea."

I stopped gooping. "Care to tell me why we're doomed for failure?"

"Do you really want to know why?"

The gleam in his eyes should've warned me off. But I was past that point.

"Yes, I do."

"Because you can't kiss me the way you do and tell me you're into Gregor."

"This kiss was business. And I didn't kiss you. You kissed me." I went back to gooping. Handling the wall repair material, literally from hell, was safer.

"Would you like to test that theory?"

He was mocking me, and it still made my insides get tingly.

"You need to stop. You only want me because you think I'm one of your toys, and you don't like other people playing with your toys. I'm not your toy."

He leaned in closer. "Does that mean I can't play with you?"

Why did that shoot like a heat-seeking missile to every sexual organ in my body? I grabbed my bucket and stepped away from him.

"There will be no playing."

"No playing at all? Because you're right. If I can't play

with you, I'm not going to take well to others playing with you."

"I'll play with whomever I choose." I dropped the bucket by his feet, ducked under his arm, and walked away. I'd hike back down alone.

28

I pulled out my notepad, skimming through the names. I still needed to get back to Zark's and ask some of the people there. If they all said yes, I might still be short on references.

"How many do you have?" Zab asked, pulling a chair over to my desk.

"Thirty-five." I'd numbered each name.

"We're running out of time. We're down to days, not weeks." Zab sighed, leaning an elbow on the desk as he looked it over. "I'm sorry I couldn't get more. I'm surprised at how many people hesitated to stand up as a reference when I asked."

"I get it. They don't want to get in the middle of a fight if they don't have to, and it's easier to say no to you than me." Everyone in Xest knew if they stood up as a reference for me, they were definitely choosing a side. As someone who'd hung out in the shadows most of her life, it was completely relatable. It didn't help matters any, but it was hard to condemn them for something I'd done myself.

Staying out of the fray had been my life goal before I'd gotten to Xest.

"Still, I feel like I'm letting you down." He tapped the page. "We should check with Bibbi and Musso. I'm sure they'll help out."

I shook my head, closing the book. "I don't want to ask them yet. If they say no, it's awkward, since I see them every day."

"But you need the numbers," Zab said, then yelled toward the back room, "Musso, Bibbi!"

"Zab..." I said, my words dying as the two of them walked out of the back room.

"Will you stand up as references for Tippi at her immigration appointment?" Zab asked, ignoring my glowering.

Musso squinted, as if he didn't understand the question, and my stomach felt like it was doing a triple loop. This was what I'd been afraid of. Dammit. Now it was going to be weird here.

Musso crossed the room to stand in front of my desk. "You already asked us weeks ago. Why don't you already have us on the list?"

"Yeah, I said yes when she still hated me," Bibbi asked.

I turned to Zab. "I guess when you said you were sure, you really were sure." I jabbed Zab in the arm, laughing. A sudden idea stole all the laughter. "You didn't say anything to Hawk, right?"

"I'm not an *idiot*. You'd kill me, and you're getting better at magic, so you might be able to do it, thanks to me." He smiled, polishing his nails on his shirt.

"I am, right? I mean, getting better at magic."

"Yeah, you've haven't blown anything up once. I'm even thinking maybe you could send your own newsflashes soon."

The image of a giant dragon in the square had us both shaking our heads a couple of seconds later.

"Maybe not yet," I said.

"Yeah, let's wait a little longer."

Musso came in the back room, where I was making a tea.

"You going to meet your friend tonight?" Musso asked, coming to make tea beside me.

Jeans and a snug sweater didn't scream date. Yes, maybe I had used a little bit of lip gloss, but my lips were dry. It wasn't for Gregor, even if I was seeing him. I needed names for my list, and looking a little a cuter wasn't going to hurt my cause.

"I'm going to Zark's, but not to see Gregor. Need to try to get more names. Why?"

"No reason," he said with a shrug, in a tone that begged for a follow-up. Musso didn't talk that much, and when he did, there was always something in his head.

"Musso, I've never had to drag information out of you before. Don't make me do it now."

Teacup in his hand, he turned to me as if contemplating his words as he eyed me up. "It's not quite the right moment for this conversation."

Hawk had gotten to him and now I was going to get the same evasive reasoning?

"It's the exact right time for this conversation."

"I don't think this Gregor boy is right for you."

I knew it. I didn't say it aloud, but in my head I was screaming it from the mountaintops.

"Why is that?" I asked. Hawk was written all over this. What was he saying about Gregor?

"Couldn't tell you, except to say I've been around a

long time, and sometimes you sense things. I know you're young and have to figure it out on your own, but you asked."

Why had I asked? I took my tea, about to go back to my desk, when it occurred to me that I might not agree on Gregor, but Musso was right. He had been around a long time.

I glanced toward the door, making sure no one was about to wander in. "Musso, is there a way to find out information about past citizens of Xest?"

"Why? Who are you curious about? Xest isn't that large. I've probably talked to most of the people here at some point."

"I was wondering about my mother. I'm pretty sure she came from here, or at least visited."

"Your last name is Tudor, right? I don't recall anyone with that name." He took a seat on the couch, leaning back as if it helped him think.

"That name might've been made up, but her first name was Jossi."

He folded his arms behind his head and rocked back in his chair, staring at the ceiling. "Hmm. That doesn't ring a bell. What level was she?"

"I don't know for sure, but I'd guess a Whimsy at most." As diligently as she'd tried to hide my magic, she'd never worn a necklace or marred her own skin. Had she left Xest because she'd run out of magic? It was possible, although it seemed that most of them didn't make it out in time.

"A lot of Whimsy witches don't make it far from the factory. I might not have met her then. Why are you asking now?" he asked.

"No reason."

Whatever that thing was in the Unsettled Lands, it hated me. It hated me before the wall, even. It felt personal, and I couldn't understand why.

29

"Tippi!"

I turned, realizing Gregor was behind me. "How long have you been back there?" I waited for him to catch up with me.

He was breathing heavily by the time he got to me. "I've been calling you for the last ten minutes or so. You didn't seem to hear me. Where you heading? You want some company?"

I glanced in the direction of the wall, where I'd been heading. It wasn't like that huge thing was a secret. Everyone in Xest knew about the wall, as evidenced by the great divide it caused, but I still hesitated. What if he came and saw all the black goop, then asked me about the black goop? What was it? Where did it come from? People around here already disliked me. I couldn't imagine that information would add to my fan base.

Gregor was still staring at me, waiting for an answer.

"Yeah, sure." In spite of having no gloves, I rubbed sweaty hands on the backs of my legs.

"Do you come up this way a lot?" he asked, climbing beside me.

"Just when I want to get some exercise." I walked a little faster so he couldn't see my face as I lied. I'd gotten better at it, but I wasn't going to win an award anytime soon.

"Do you go check the wall?" he asked. "I've heard there were some problems with it."

I hesitated a second and then continued. The cracks were probably common knowledge as well, even though I hadn't heard most people talk about them. Gregor was on the same side, though, and he worked at Zark's. He probably heard everything.

"I'm sorry. I didn't mean to pry. I just wanted you to know that I'd help with it if I could. If you wanted to tell me what you were thinking of doing, you know. I didn't think it was a secret."

"No, it's definitely not. I don't know, I guess I just don't like talking about it." Now that was the truth if anyone ever spoke it.

Instead of heading to the places with the recent repairs, I stopped at the first clearing, a ways shy of the wall.

"Want me to start a fire? Hang out for a little bit?" Gregor asked, already piling up a couple twigs and lighting them.

They were getting to me. I was letting Hawk, and now Musso, turn me against Gregor for no reason. Hawk had probably recruited Musso, and here I was, getting all weird with Gregor. Either way, I didn't really have time to hang out, but now I didn't want to tell him that. Hawk would not dictate my life.

"You know, I've got to get going. I've got some appointments, but maybe we can hang out tomorrow?"

"Yeah, definitely. I'll walk you back."

"My meeting isn't in town, but I'll catch up with you tomorrow," I said, giving him a wave and heading off before he tried to follow me.

It was true, I did have an appointment, and it wasn't something that would be Gregor-compatible.

I took several deep breaths and focused, letting the cool air wash over me. Feeling centered, head clear, I shook out my hands and prepared myself. Bautere didn't typically give me warning. I'd need to sense him before he struck.

"You look like you're waiting to be attacked," Hawk said.

"Did you follow me?" Was everyone following me today? Or had he been following Gregor, who'd been following me? Either way, I was going to have to find a different place to practice.

"You're extremely easy to find. You might as well draw big arrows pointing in the direction you went."

It didn't escape me that he hadn't denied or admitted following me.

"Who have you been practicing with up here? That's what you're getting ready to do, isn't it? You know, I would help you with that little problem." He leaned against a nearby tree and casually crossed his arms, his jacket flapping in the cold air, not that it ever seemed to get to him.

"Thank you, but no. I'm doing quite well on my own."

"Excited to see the progress."

"I'm not performing today, so you can be on your way."

Even as I spoke, it was already clear he wouldn't leave. When did Hawk do anything I'd asked? Never.

"Show me. What's the problem?" he asked, walking closer and then circling me.

"I do this the way I want. Not the way you tell me."

"Then make me go away," he said, walking in front of me, his toes brushing mine.

The hard look in his eyes started to switch to something else with a lot more heat. He moved his hand to my cheek, touching my face.

My heart began to pound, and I turned my face away.

"Stop touching me. All you do lately is touch me. People from Xest don't touch. I shouldn't have to be the one to tell you that."

"Some people do," he said.

Only people who were intimate, and we wouldn't be that. He'd taken a bunch of boulders and blocked off that road completely.

I stepped back before I could stop myself, before I could convince myself that I didn't do that anymore. That I didn't retreat. That wasn't who I was going to be, ever again. It was the first time I'd relinquished my space to him in a while, but it had to be done for my own sanity. He'd used me up every which way before I left, and I had nothing left to give. He'd take it all if he had his way. He'd lost Belinda, and now he wanted me to take her place in and out of bed, and that couldn't happen.

"We aren't *those* people," I said, trying to hold firm to my spot, refusing to retreat again, even in the face of his onslaught.

"What if we were?" he asked. As if he were sorting this out himself.

He didn't even know what he wanted. There was that same confused look in his face, the one I'd seen after he kissed me the first time, like he couldn't figure out why he wanted me.

It was the very thing I needed to shore up my resolve.

"I'm done for the day," I said, my tone making it clear I was done in more ways than one.

"Pretend I'm your enemy and do your worst," he said, leaning in closer.

"You kicked me out of Xest, you stopped me from getting a job and took my apartment. I don't have to *pretend* anything."

"Then what's the problem?"

"I don't want to practice with you."

"Then don't hold back."

It was too good of an offer to turn down.

I nodded and took a couple of steps back. Without warning, I leapt at him, trying to get a good angle on him and land a blow to his side. He caught me in midair, dragging us both to the ground. It was one of my worst showings yet. No matter how angry I was, it wouldn't translate into action.

He landed underneath me and then quickly rolled on top, the length of him pressing into me. My hands were pressed to his chest in between us as he reached down, cupping my face.

I'd touched enough people with magic at this point to realize a couple of things. The first was that Hawk was stronger than I'd initially realized. Much stronger. Second, something about our magic was compatible in a way that didn't make me comfortable. Even now, as he was touching me, I could feel mine forming some sort of bond with his, like it wanted to be woven together.

Logically, everything screamed to stay away from him. But physically? It was like we gravitated to each other and nothing could stop the draw.

"Let me up," I said, hoping he'd take the fluster on my skin and the huskiness of my voice for exertion and not the want I felt for him on the most basic level.

"When you insisted on staying in Xest, I let it go. I didn't force the issue when I could've dragged you back to Salem. When you took a job at Zark's, I let it go even though I detested the spectacle."

He paused, dropping his head, but I could see his jaw shift. He seemed to realign himself and looked at me again.

"I've let many things go. But if you're going to show up with fresh bruises every day and think I'm not going to get involved, you're wrong."

Stuck in the snow with Hawk leaning over me, pinning me to the ground. Our flesh tingling where it connected, and other parts warming when they shouldn't.

My motto had been to never back down, never run. Considering I was literally stuck with my back on the ground, today was going to have to be considered a throw-out, or at least an exception to the rule. New mottos or not, I'd lost.

And how easily he'd beaten me riled me up like nothing else. Using my magic to try to dislodge him was a joke when all it wanted to do was wrap itself around him and purr like a kitten. If I tried to show him my teeth, with my luck, I'd probably give him a love bite.

"Well? What will it be?" he asked.

He was waiting for me to answer as his gaze shifted

from my eyes to my lips, his body molded slightly closer to mine, and the heat growing in me alone might make a puddle right where I lay in the snow.

If he didn't move soon, there was only one place this was heading, and there was no guarantee I'd push him off, even if I should be.

"Fine. You want to see how I'm practicing? Be my guest." This would be even better, because he was going to hate it.

His gaze moved from my lips to my eyes. "Chicken."

Chicken? This from the man who looked at me as if I'd committed some capital crime after he'd kissed me? I didn't know what his game was, but I wanted no part of it. It was bad enough that our lives were so entangled again.

He got up and offered me a hand. I nearly jumped to my feet unaided. I was light as a feather without him weighing me down.

He watched as I got back to my feet. "Since you clearly aren't any better at defending yourself against me, what have you been doing to earn those bruises?"

"She typically does very well, Hawk—not that you could tell from that performance," Bautere said as he stepped out of the woods.

"Bautere." Hawk's jaw clenched before he turned his full attention to Bautere. In that moment, I saw the fury of hell shining through. It looked like he was the first of the four horsemen coming to scorch the earth.

"You've been training her?" Hawk asked, closing the gap between them.

"She was eager and I saw promise," Bautere said, holding his ground.

Hawk glanced at me for just a second, but something

in Bautere's words seemed to appease him slightly. "You cause any permanent damage and you answer to me."

Bautere raised his chin. "I'm not looking to maim the person who might be our only hope."

"Just so we're on the same page."

"I believe we are." Bautere nodded toward me. "Perhaps we should skip today."

I nodded. Going into full-blown combat training in front of Hawk did not seem like a good idea when there was steam nearly coming out of his ears.

Bautere nodded at Hawk and then turned, leaving us alone.

With nothing else to do, I headed back to the broker's office. Hawk followed. Neither of us spoke much on the way.

It wasn't until we got inside, and I was headed toward the back stairs, that he said, "Did you just stroll up and ask him for help? Do you know that his kind eat humans like you?"

No, actually, I didn't know that, and wouldn't admit it now. "I brought him an offering." His words sank a little deeper into my head. "And what do you mean, humans like me? Do you think you're above *us* somehow?"

"Do you have any idea how many he's killed?"

"I seem to be quite healthy. I did what I had to, and I learned. You have no right to criticize the way I handle my business."

"You could've gotten yourself killed. You're so focused on why you shouldn't trust me that you're blind to everything else."

I headed toward the back stairs again. He could go wherever he pleased, which was probably straight to hell, where he'd be with his own kind. Actually, that was an idea. He should hook up with Mertie if he was in the market.

"Tippi."

I took another step before I stopped, pausing to hear what he wanted, because I couldn't bring myself to completely stop caring.

"I don't want to fight with you," he said, sounding almost as tired as I was.

It was something, an olive branch of sorts, even if it was a little late.

"Neither do I, but you don't give me a choice."

I opened the door, giving him a nod of acknowledgment before I went upstairs.

30

I was sitting at my desk when Hawk walked out of the back room, Oscar following behind. Hawk kept walking as Oscar stopped in front of my desk.

"You might want to come along for this," Oscar said.

"Why? What's wrong?" Hawk was already out the door as I got to my feet.

"You'll see when you get there," Oscar said. He followed Hawk out as I ran and grabbed my jacket, hurrying to catch up.

Oscar was squinting, scanning the area as I caught up to him. Hawk was far ahead, and there was an air about him that instinctively said he wanted his space. People on the street noticed too, stopping and watching our procession.

"Where are we going?" I asked Oscar.

"Zark's."

"Why?"

Oscar shook his head, his devil-may-care attitude replaced by an expression that made me wonder if there were a demon about to hunt us down. "It's best if you hear for yourself."

I swallowed that as well as I would a few stones with a chaser of bad milk, and it all fell into a sour lump in my belly. It wasn't the fight that I feared we were walking into that rattled me. I'd had enough brawls with enough magical creatures that a few bruises meant nothing. With Oscar and Hawk beside me, I'd probably live. Not to toot our own horn, but the three of us combined were a formidable trio. My fear, the gurgling in my gut, was about *why* Hawk was heading into a fight.

He didn't get mad and stalk others down like this. He was more of a kill-them-in-cold-blood type, and nothing about him was cold right now. I could feel the steam coming off him from way back here.

I didn't beg Oscar for more information, though. He wasn't going to talk, and I'd know soon enough anyway. With Zark's already in sight, I needed the next few minutes to gather myself for whatever was about to come.

Hawk disappeared into Zark's. He was already at the bar, speaking to Zark, when we followed.

Zark glanced at us as we walked in.

"I'm not here about Tippi—or not her job, anyway," Hawk said, looking my way. He was giving me a feeling like someone had tied cement blocks to my ankles and tried to dump me overboard. What had gone down that was going to screw me so bad that I didn't know about? I might've missed the cinder blocks, but the stones in my stomach were growing in size.

"What is it, then?" Zark asked.

Hawk turned back to Zark. Oscar moved a little closer to my side. He wasn't touching me, but he seemed to think I might need support.

"I need to talk to your son," Hawk said.

That was all I needed to hear. Hawk had never liked Gregor, and I was not going to be a party to some witch hunt. Sort of fitting, since I was in Xest, a place filled with witches.

The old man straightened up and lost all of his soft edges. "Why? What business do you have with Gregor?"

Yeah, that was what I'd like to know as well.

"He's working with the other side," Hawk said.

"Bull. Not my son." Zark's chest puffed up as he turned his head, yelling to the back, "Gregor, get out here."

Hawk might like to stick it to me out of amusement, but even he wouldn't go this far to give me a bad day. Hawk wanted to think the worst of Gregor, had since the moment we'd become friends. He might know something, but that didn't mean it was correct.

No, this was ending now. I wouldn't let him string up my buddy because he didn't like others to play with his toys. I stepped away from Oscar and placed myself in between Hawk and the door that led to the back. If Hawk wanted Gregor, he'd have to go through me. I might not be as good at protecting myself, but I could protect others pretty damned well, maybe even from Hawk.

"Step out of the way," Hawk said.

I didn't budge. "I know you don't like him, but you need to leave Gregor alone. He's done nothing to you, and whatever you might have imagined, it's not true."

"I said, step out of the way."

"No." Magic was boiling up in me, fizzing though my body like I was going to blow.

Gregor walked into the main room, all the patrons in the place now paying keen attention to what was going down. I wanted to kill Hawk for pulling a stunt like this.

Just the implication of what he was suggesting would tarnish Gregor's reputation for a decade.

I was standing my ground in between them when Hawk reached down and grabbed me by the waist. I grabbed his arms, letting him get a feel of my magic and what I was going to do if he didn't unhand me. Instead of feeling anything, he picked me up and deposited me back down beside Oscar. I scurried back to the front, not quite a buffer anymore.

"What's going on?" Gregor asked. The tension in the room was palpable as everyone waited to see if there was a traitor in our midst. Which there *wasn't*, and I couldn't wait until Gregor proved it.

"Oscar picked up a trace of your magic at the newest crack in the wall. The one we repaired that's already failing."

"It's failing?" I asked Hawk, torn between outrage for Gregor and fear for what was going to happen to Xest.

Hawk nodded. "Found it this morning."

I suddenly felt like I was a hundred pounds heavier. I needed to go look, but I couldn't yet, not until I made sure Hawk didn't kill Gregor.

I would stand up to Hawk in a way no one else seemed willing to do. I couldn't just run out of here right now.

"It might be breaking, but your info is wrong. Gregor walked up that way with me the other day. He started us a fire. That's probably what you picked up on. He's not working with *them*." At least a thread of reasoning, even if it was weak. They hadn't made something up out of thin air.

Hawk's gaze was on me, as if he were furious I was interfering and sad for me all at once. It wasn't a combination I was used to seeing on him. On the average day, he was just pissed off at me for various reasons.

He turned to Gregor. "Are you going to admit it or have her defend your lies? Are you going to tell her you sabotaged the repair? At least be man enough to stand up for yourself."

I edged farther in between them. It would be safer that way when Gregor told Hawk to go to hell. Hawk was being an ass, but there was no need for bloodshed. Ultimately we were all on the same side, even if some people seemed to keep forgetting that.

I stood there, ready, but Gregor wasn't talking. Why wasn't he talking? Gregor was never short on words.

I turned around, and Gregor's gaze met mine. It veered off almost as fast, as if he couldn't quite look me in the eye.

I turned to Hawk, who never had a problem meeting my gaze, as if he could offer some clarification on what was happening. Was Hawk right? Had Gregor betrayed him, me, everyone who was fighting to keep that evil from contaminating all of Xest? And when had I started relying on Hawk's word for it? The last one was easy. As soon as Gregor couldn't look at me.

Hawk gave a single shake of his head, confirming what my gut and Gregor's silence was already saying.

I had a mile-long list of questions, the first being the most important. Why wasn't Gregor at least trying to defend himself? There had to be some reason.

"Why aren't you speaking?" Zark asked, beating me to it.

It was a good thing, because my words didn't seem to want to form. They'd been smothered by shock and the startling feeling of betrayal.

Only silence filled the room.

I turned back to Gregor, slowly, almost afraid to see his face and the guilt that was going to be written there as my mind ran back over all the things that should've been obvious to me. The signs had been there. The questions. He'd always been so quick with them, squirreling away little tidbits. I'd pushed unease away, over and over again, and now it was flooding up around me, drowning me.

Gregor wasn't my friend. He was another liar.

"Speak, dammit. Are you working with them? Are you with them?" his father asked. Zark, unfortunately, was still looking for more clarification.

As surely as my heart was bruised and bleeding, Zark's was bleeding out. The weight of Gregor's betrayal seemed to be bringing this formerly hard man to his knees.

I wanted to wrap my arms around Zark and say it would be okay, but it wouldn't be. His son was on the other side, and this wasn't like a political fight in Rest. This was for all the marbles. If the other side won this war, Xest wouldn't be recognizable.

"Yes. I'm working with them. I'm sorry if you can't understand the beauty of what's growing there, but you're trying to kill something that's a miracle," Gregor said, his voice rising as he spoke.

The door to Zark's opened and Raydam stepped inside, followed by Belinda and others I recognized from their sneers on the street.

The rest of the patrons in Zark, who'd only been watching on before, also stood. It was a packed house, and not in a good way. This was the first time today I'd actually wondered if our fearsome trio would be fierce enough. I could handle some bruises, but this might turn out to be something way worse.

Gregor paused for only a few seconds before he said, "I'm sorry," and moved to stand with his people.

Zark looked at the newcomers and then back to Gregor. He leaned a hand on the bar, his shoulders dropping, as he watched his son join the other side.

"You should leave. You're not welcome here," Hawk said, when Zark didn't seem to have the strength.

Without a last look back, they left.

The room exhaled. Zark deflated as some of the patrons went over, trying to console him.

Hawk walked out, and I followed, simply because I wanted to get away from the crowd. I'd thought I'd shed most of my softness, but another bit of fluff had been torn from me today.

I stopped, watching as the group walked away. Gregor turned, taking a few steps back toward me, even as Hawk stood not far from my back.

"Tippi, can I talk to you?" he asked.

"Did you sabotage my repair?" I asked, needing to hear him say it.

Palms up, he lifted his hands slightly. "Yes, but it's—"

"Then no. I don't want to talk to you now. Maybe not ever."

I turned from him and began walking in the other direction.

"Tippi," Gregor called.

"You're lucky you're still breathing. Now walk away," Hawk said, getting into his normal controlling mode and stopping Gregor from following me. This time, there would be no fight about it.

31

"You're going to have to ask Hawk," Oscar said, and then slid a shot in front of me. He typically wouldn't be caught dead in Zab's favorite bar, but these were special circumstances, and it was the only place Hawk wouldn't be.

"He's right. Just bring it up to him. You don't have the numbers, and now you're down another with Gregor," Zab said, tapping the pad with his pencil. He took his shot and slid that one in front of me too. "It'll make the prospect more bearable."

"I see the way he looks at you. He'll definitely do it for you," Bibbi said, keeping *most* of the melancholy out of her tone. She looked at her drink, and then the others that were just placed in front of me.

"I don't need another," I said. I threw back one of the shots, and then took a second as it lit my throat on fire. I should've remembered Oscar saying something called lava was his favorite drink.

I looked at the three people sitting there, all egging me on. "You really think he'll do it?"

"He'll do it. He's not going to bring it up, but he'll do it," Zab said.

"Not that I blame him, really," Oscar added. "I mean, you sing 'You Don't Own Me' anytime he's around, like it's your theme song."

I shook my head right before I tossed the second shot back. Zab's shot was much better and an easier recovery. "The monkeys like that song. I can't help it if I sing now and then."

"And why do the monkeys play it?" Oscar asked, laughing.

It was becoming well known that they had some strange inclination to add theme songs to every part of my life. They also seemed to have a gift of knowing the right tune for the moment—usually. I wouldn't fault them for it.

"Whatever. Hawk's as guilty as I am because he acts like he owns me. A reminder isn't out of hand."

"You need another?" Oscar asked, starting to raise his hand to signal the bartender.

"No. I need to be coherent tonight." I got up from the table before I was incapable of it, and they all assumed I was going to find Hawk. There was something else I had to do first. "See you guys tomorrow."

I knelt beside the repair that was cracking, running my hand over it. Black chunks fell out at the softest touch, dusting my hand and dropping to the ground. It was the first time I'd seen the damage to the repair. I hadn't checked the other spots yet, but I was sure they were the same.

It was seeping out of the break—trying to wrap its evil around me, trying to tell me how much it despised me.

"You're not going to win," I whispered, in case it was listening.

A branch crunched, and I swung around, knowing it wasn't Hawk. He'd never be so clunky as to announce his arrival that way.

Gregor walked toward me and then slowed his steps as I stared back. I might not have known what to say, but what I felt must have shown. His eyes jerked down for a moment. I gave him my back, focusing my attention on the failing repair and hoping he'd leave if I ignored him.

"I wasn't using you," he said.

My reply was silence.

"I care about you. I still care about you. Tippi, won't you please talk to me?"

He was whining, after the lies and telling me he wanted to help repair the wall. As much as I wanted to ignore his presence, it was just too much to stay silent through.

"You want to make this right? Tell me what you did to the repair." Whatever it was, he hadn't done it alone. He was too weak. He'd had help, and I could easily guess who from. How many lies had there been between us? Had any part of our relationship been real?

When I didn't get an answer, I turned away from him again.

Then he was there, standing in front of me, making himself unavoidable.

I tried anyway, walking a good ten feet away. He followed me, dogging my steps. My fists curled as his offer to help continued to haunt me. I'd *kissed* this man.

"Stop following me. There's nothing to talk about. All you want is information to use against me anyway."

"I wasn't just using you. I still want to be with you."

He wasn't *just* using me. How nice to know.

"I don't want to be with you, so you should leave. Now."

"Tippi, please hear me out. That's all I'm asking."

He wouldn't stop following me, no matter how many times I glared or how fast I walked. The easiest way to be done with this situation was to go through it, which meant hearing him out. I'd let him get it all off his chest, and then tell him it didn't matter, because it didn't. Our friendship had been a lie from start to finish.

I spun and threw my hands up. "Fine. Go ahead and tell me, then. Get it off your chest, and after you're done, if I don't want to hear anymore, you leave. That's the deal."

He nodded quickly. "I wasn't trying to date you because they told me to. I wanted to date you because I *liked* you."

It just kept getting worse.

"So they asked you to date me?"

"If I hadn't liked you, I would've said no. What does it matter if they suggested it?"

Of course it mattered, and not for a second would he have contemplated saying no to them, even if he hadn't liked me. But the more I asked and interrupted, the longer this would carry on. My patience could barely handle it already. I remained silent, my chest heaving with the struggle to remain calm.

"I thought as we got close, I could make you see what a beautiful thing is growing here. You'd come to understand how wrong you are. I know it because I believe in you."

If I had a gun right now, I might've put myself out of

my misery. He believed in me? The lost, wayward one who didn't see the error of her ways? How had I been so foolish? Actually, I knew *that* answer. He'd talked a good game. He'd told me everything I wanted to hear. Add to that, Hawk kept warning me off, and damned if I didn't like to spite him.

"Gregor, you have zero idea what you're talking about. You'll always want to let that thing out, and I'll never stop fighting it because it's disgusting and evil." And then I added, in the same condescending tone he'd used, "I really wish I could've helped you see the error of your ways, but I guess it's not meant to be."

He nodded. "Then I guess that's it," he said, sounding as angry as I was now.

"Yes. That's it."

"I'm sorry it has to end this way."

"So am I."

Gregor had said all the right things, acted the right way, but he couldn't have been more wrong. He might believe that he'd been truly interested in me, but he'd been more intrigued by being the man who would turn me, make me into the person he thought I should be.

Could I truly fault him when, in essence, I'd done the same? I'd never wanted him. I'd only toyed with the idea when I thought he was the man I *should* want. We'd both been trying to fit square pegs into round holes. With nothing left to say, I turned away from him, ready to walk away from whatever shred of truth we'd had.

But there wouldn't be any walking away, not today. While I'd been so preoccupied letting him have his say, they'd been laying a trap for me. Now it was too late.

I could already feel the pull of magic before I spotted them. Raydam appeared first, then Belinda, then four other nameless faces I'd seen sneering at me. They came from each side, all with their palms up, and I could feel the magical fence forming around me.

I'd have said anything not to have to dredge through the black hole of emotions that might have been at the heart of the problem.

I was here, all by myself and doomed to fail, just the way Gregor knew I would, because I'd so stupidly confided in him that I was lousy at protecting myself. So what had they done? The same thing I would've—waited until I was alone.

I looked back at Gregor.

"How could you?"

"We're both doing what we think is right. If you're not here, this wall will eventually fail. There was no choice but to use you."

"You would say that, wouldn't you?" I let out a little huff of breath. Why was it that weak people always blamed their victims? I'd walked away from him too soon. I should've punched him in the face first.

Gregor's cheeks turned red. "I told them I could turn you to our side. I *protected* you. Why do you think no one touched you? Because of *me*. I'm the strong one. But you just won't stop. No matter how horrible he is. He stole your home, he kicked you out of Xest, and you still helped him."

"You're wrong. I'm not doing this for him. I'm doing this for me, because whatever lies beyond my wall? It's evil. And that you can't feel it?" I shook my head.

"They were right. You can't be saved."

I was surrounded, but they'd been smart. They'd only brought enough people to ensure a win. If half of Xest disappeared, that might tip people off that something was up.

I turned to Belinda. If this was going down, I wasn't holding anything back. I was laying it all out there before I died.

"You've been waiting a long time to get me, haven't you? Just couldn't stand that he didn't want you. That he'd rather keep me around and didn't give a shit about how you felt. You were nothing to him."

She lunged at me, but Raydam grabbed her arm. "No. We do this together. She'll get the end she deserves."

They circled. And then I realized Gregor was inside the circle with me, but he was looking at his companions as if he weren't supposed to be there.

"What are you doing?" he asked. He tried to approach Raydam but got stopped short by whatever magic had formed.

"We need an anchor," Raydam said.

"What are you talking about? Not me. I helped you. I'm one of you." Gregor pounded on the invisible barricade.

"If you truly believe in this cause, you'd be willing to give your life for it. You took the vow."

"Raydam, don't do this to me, please," Gregor said, getting to his knees.

No one responded as they began chanting. A molten red haze began to form around us, slowly growing brighter and hotter. They were going to cook us alive.

"They're going to kill us," Gregor said, looking at me stunned. "Can you do something?"

"Oh, yeah, sure. Now we're a team? I guess when it was just me it wasn't such a problem." Sarcasm probably wasn't the best use of my energy right now, but sometimes it felt unavoidable.

Still, he was right. We were going to die. When I'd been in a similar situation with Zab, my instincts had taken over. I looked to Gregor, who was definitely going to die with me, and there was no bubbling magic building within, ready to take on the bad guys. I was as flat as I'd accused Hawk of being.

None of the charms and lower-level stuff I'd been practicing with Zab was going to work. None of my newfound skills from Bautere were going to get us out of this magic roaster they were constructing.

Gregor was circling, frenzied and useless.

"Give me something to work with. Tell me you need to live or something," I said, scrambling for some tingle of magic to take over me.

"I do. I want to live. I have to live. I'm too young," he said, falling on his knees in front of me now.

It did nothing, not even a hiccup.

"Give me something not *you* related."

"The wall. They think once they kill you, the wall will be destroyed with you and free *it*. Isn't that how you supposedly built it in the first place?"

Bingo. A wave of magic surged through me instantly. I raised my hands, shooting it toward their wall. A blast as loud as a bomb filled the air, and then a buzzing muted all the noise. A blinding light filled the sky, and I was knocked off my feet by my own magic.

I woke with my cheek in the snow and an opaque, swirling blue dome all around me. Utterly drained, I pushed myself into a sitting position and looked around at the small area, probably no bigger than thirty feet in diameter.

Gregor was lying on the ground not far from me, and there was a glowing black stone in the center. I got to my feet, laid a hand on it, and jerked back. It was *it*. This dome was acting as a field around it, containing it from the outside. But I was on the inside with it this time. How had I done that?

I moved over to Gregor, who was curled on his side. Everything he'd done had walked him into this position, and yet it was hard to see him right now, curled on his side, too weak to stand.

"You idiot. You chose them, and they didn't even give a shit about you."

I didn't know if he'd taken a bad blow or what, but he wasn't getting up. He wasn't bleeding, but he looked like death on closer perusal.

I knelt down, putting a couple of fingers to his wrist to gauge how strong his pulse and magic were. Both were barely there.

"Gregor, what's wrong with you?"

"I've got nothing left." He turned onto his back, but it seemed to take everything he had, and there was still no sign of a visible wound. "They took all my magic. Every last drop."

"During that... Whatever that chanting was?"

He nodded, but just slightly.

"Why am I okay, then? Why didn't they take mine?"

"You're too strong. They couldn't."

I should've hated the guy. On some level I still did, and yet it was hard to hate anyone enough to want to see them like this. After all, he'd believed in what he was doing, as I had. We just believed in something different. That shouldn't have made us enemies, but it had.

"We'll get you out of here. You can go to Rest." I couldn't jump puddles, but I'd go into hock to Hawk if need be. He'd have no reason not to help, since Gregor was effectively neutralized anyway.

He shook his head. "I won't make it that long."

I walked over to the opaque dome that enclosed us and laid my hands on it, trying to push through. It felt like pushing on the side of a mountain. I shoved harder, knowing it wouldn't work.

I laid my hands on it again, this time feeling for its magical signature. There were too many to count. It was me, Belinda, Raydam, even *it*.

What kind of monstrosity had I made? I couldn't get us out, not even to save Gregor's life. I definitely wasn't going to be able to save myself. I'd signed my own death warrant.

"Tippi," Gregor called.

I went and knelt beside him again. "I'm working on it. I'll come up with something."

"Please, tell my father I'm sorry. I never wanted to hurt him."

"You'll be..."

He shook his head, using the last of his strength to grab my hand. "I'm dead, Tippi. Just promise me you'll tell him."

"I will." The image of Zark's heart breaking as Gregor had left him at the bar was burned in my mind.

His hand went slack as his eyelids drooped. I settled down next to him, listening to the death rattle in his chest.

32

I'd tried every piece of magic I'd learned and more that I'd made up. Nothing worked. The only thing I could guess was that I'd hijacked the dome they'd been creating around me, and then somehow sucked *it* inside.

Too bad I didn't have anyone to bounce my theory off. I wasn't sure how many hours I'd been here, but Gregor's body was cold. When I put my fingers to his wrist, there was no pulse. Worse, there wasn't a tingle of magic either. Gregor was gone, and suddenly all I could think about were the laughs we'd had, like his death had swept clean his betrayal for the moment.

I grazed my hand over his, feeling utterly alone, only to be jerked to an awareness. There was a thundering sound on the other side of the dome prison. I jumped to my feet, heading toward the noise.

A clawed hand broke through the dome. I scrambled back to the other side. They were sending something in here to kill me. This was it. I'd need to fight my way past whatever monster was coming for me. Another claw broke through, before the head of a monster appeared, all teeth and horns, growling as it fought its way in.

I should attack it now, before it finished its entry, while it was still struggling. I didn't have a weapon other than my magic, and it would have to be enough. I had to do it. Its waist was through. I had to attack before it freed its legs. I'd trained with Bautere for just this moment. If I didn't use the skills now, there would never be another chance.

I leapt in the air, trying to angle myself so that I'd come down on top of its shoulders. I'd wrap my arms around its neck and choke it out.

I flew toward it, but the creature was too fast. It ducked, and I skimmed over it. I landed with a thump on the ground. I was dazed, but not from the fall. I looked down at my hand, the one that had grazed the creature, doubting what I'd felt.

I turned, staring at its fangs and roughened skin, and saw a familiar glimmer in the eyes.

"Hawk?"

It growled in response. Oh yeah, that was definitely Hawk. I got up, running over.

"What are you doing? You've got to get out of here. Go back the other way. You'll get stuck." I pushed on his shoulders, but there was no moving him where he didn't want to go.

He continued to push his way in, finally dropping to the ground inside the dome in spite of me.

"Why did you do that? You idiot!"

The creature's body was slowly morphing until the familiar form of Hawk was lying in the snow, completely naked. I definitely wasn't dead yet, because I had a hard time not appreciating his form. He rolled to his back, not a shy bone in him.

I purposely kept my gaze on his chest and face.

Damn, it slipped lower. But whoa. He really didn't have any reason to be shy.

Face. Stare at his face.

By the time my gaze did make it to his face, he'd raised a brow. I'd just gotten caught sneaking a peek.

"I was checking for injuries, you egomaniac," I said.

"Sure you were," he said, amusement oozing out.

"Why did you do that, anyway? Are you insane?"

"I couldn't break you out. Nothing else worked but forcing my way in," he said, still a bit winded from the effort. "The force is stronger going outward. This dome has a weird gravitational pull of some sort."

"Then why? Now you're stuck. You'll die with me. There's no way out of this." I wanted to leap on top of his still-reclined form and pound on his chest for the stupidity.

"You'll get us out," he said with utter confidence.

"I couldn't save myself or him," I said, pointing to Gregor's dead body.

Hawk looked to the body and then back at me. "I'm not worried."

Of all the egomaniacal head trips. Of course Hawk would think I could move mountains for him alone. There were no bounds to his arrogance, even now.

"That's why you came in here? You figured that I wouldn't be able to save myself, but I'd save *you*? We've been at each other's throats since I got back, and yet you think I'll find the will to get you out?"

"Yes," he said, as if it were a simple matter of fact.

"That's insane. You tried to get me railroaded out of Xest. I couldn't get a job or a place to live. You filled my position in a day."

He laughed softly. "I knew something was bothering you that day when you wouldn't tell me. I didn't replace you. I hired someone to do a job."

"*My* job. She took my place." She even followed his every move the way I had, but he'd never get the satisfaction of hearing that from me. Not ever, not even on my deathbed, which I might be standing upon right now.

I spun, walked over to the wall, and pounded on it with both of my hands, wishing I could get out of here so I could get away from him.

"I wasn't replacing you. I didn't like seeing the empty chair where you used to sit. So I hired Bibbi. I wanted to fire her an hour after I did."

I was a horrible person, because that warmed my heart completely. I turned. "You did? Why? She's a hard worker."

"It wasn't her work. It was her. She wasn't the person who was supposed to be sitting there."

He had missed me. It didn't make any of the things he'd done any better, but at least he'd paid a price of some sort. He'd wanted me back, and fast.

I took a few steps back toward him. "If you didn't want me gone, why'd you force me out?"

He sat up a little straighter, definitely struggling more than I'd ever seen him. "Maybe I didn't want you to end up right where you are now. And perhaps part of me was worried I'd end up right where I am as well."

"Why aren't you getting up? Why do you look like you've been here longer than I have?" I asked, not liking the wrenching feeling I was getting in my gut. Hawk was a man of action. He didn't sit in times like these. He'd be up and moving around, trying to figure out a solution.

"There's another slight problem on top of not having an easy exit."

"Which is?"

He nodded toward the stone in the center as if he already knew exactly what it was. "I can feel it locked in here. There's something about *it* that's toxic to me on some level. It wasn't as bad before, but in this enclosed space with it, I'm not going to make it very long."

"Did you know that? Did you know it was in here?"

"I had my suspicions," he said, still on the ground.

"And you came?" I asked, staring at him, trying to understand such a selfless act. He could've left this dome here with me inside and been done, problem solved.

"I had to. I couldn't leave you to die." He stared back at me as if I should've known that.

I felt a tingle build within me. This time I recognized the feeling. I'd felt something similar right before I kicked a dragon's ass. All I had to do was look at Hawk, sitting there, looking drained, and it built from a tingle to a swell that washed over my body.

Hawk watched, nodding his encouragement, knowing exactly what was going to happen. If it had just been me, I would've died here. But I couldn't let him die with me.

The magic was building all around me, and I knew if I let it rise even a tiny bit more, it was going to blow the cage I'd put *it* into as well. I was about to go supernova, and *it* would be out again, worse and angrier than ever, without a wall to contain it.

"Hawk..." His name came out slightly breathless, as

most of my energy was being sucked up into the storm within.

His gaze was on me as I looked over at the cube and back to him. I could feel the magic churning all around and was barely containing it.

"Do it," Hawk said, with zero hesitation.

Did he understand? "It's going to—"

"Do. It."

I let it go, and the dome shattered all around us, blowing outward like a million shards of glass. I stood untouched, the center of the storm as Hawk rolled to his side, shielding his face.

I'd barely gotten my bearings, looking up at the sky again, when I heard a rattling noise behind me.

"Get down," Hawk yelled, right before he crashed into me, dragging me to the snow and landing on top of me. Another bomb exploded; a blast of burning air followed. A whoosh of malevolence spread out with it and leveled all the trees for a mile. A wave of dread came next as a howl filled the air and sent a shiver through me.

Hawk and I both scrambled to stand. I couldn't see it, but I could feel it swell above us like a tornado of malevolence. Hawk wrapped his hand around mine, trying to tug me behind him.

"Not this time," I said, as I stepped in front of him instead.

He gave me a short nod, but didn't let go of my hand. He wouldn't fight me on taking the lead, but I wasn't fighting alone.

I stood, feeling the anger of it all around, raging like a storm that wanted to tear down everything I was—and it couldn't. It wasn't capable. There was something about me that it couldn't attack, just like before. Just like with the grouslies it had sent. Whatever it was, whatever *I* was, it couldn't kill me. But it would kill Hawk to hurt me. If it wanted Hawk, it was going to have to come through me. I took another step toward where I felt it, letting the rage build in me.

The strange sound exploded in the air, something in between a howl of agony and an F5 tornado ready to drop upon us, before the sound and the wind was gone in an instant.

We were out, but so was it.

My shoulders slumped as I shoved my hand through my hair, twigs and leaves getting raked out as I did. I turned, looking at Hawk.

He nodded. We were both okay. We'd made it.

I looked around, surveying the damage to see Raydam, Belinda, and their small group lying dead in the snow not far from us.

"Did you kill them?" I tried not to sound too happy or relieved, even if I were both. Part of me still believed you shouldn't wish anyone dead, but them being gone made my life a lot easier. When it came down to it, it was probably always going to be me or them in the end anyway.

"No," he said. "I think you did."

Me? My hands shook. It was disarming enough to see bodies lying lifeless. Knowing you'd been the one to make them like that? Whole other level.

"How?" I asked, walking toward them.

"When they involved you in whatever they were trying to accomplish, they opened themselves up to you. You had the stronger magic and will."

The dome. I used the magic they'd been putting out to

build it, and, I guess, a little more magic than they'd planned on giving.

"Come on. We should get out of here," he said, his look mirroring the exhaustion I felt. We were both too weak right now to fend off another attack. It was time to go lick our wounds.

33

"There are forty-eight by my count," Zab said, standing beside me the morning of my immigration meeting.

Zark, Gilli, and some of her employees from the Sweet Shop were here. Musso had even brought his wife, the one I'd never met, and they were currently on the other side of the group talking to Bibbi. All Zab's friends from the Watering Hole had shown up. All the regulars from Zark's had come, including Zark himself.

"Forty-nine will be here, but I'm still short one. Maybe they won't notice?"

I'd slept almost a complete day, wasting any chance to scrounge up another person to stand up for me. After everything I'd gone through, to get kicked out for one person?

Zab glanced around again. "While you were sleeping, I told Hawk. You weren't waking up, and it had to be done. He said he's coming. Had been planning on it." He took a step away from me. "Don't hurt me."

"The only thing I want to do is hug you right now," I

said, refusing to get emotional and start crying like a big ninny.

I'd have the references for immigration. Hopefully they wouldn't blame me for wrecking a huge chunk of the Unsettled Lands. If I did get the heat for what was happening, no amount of witnesses was going to help.

"Who are you missing, then?" Zab asked.

"Don't worry. He'll be here."

The crowd went quiet as Bautere stepped through the trees. He stopped ten feet shy of the crowds, located me, and gave a nod.

"That's your forty-nine?" Zab asked. "What did you have to barter to get him to come?"

I smiled. "Nothing. He offered."

Oscar whistled as he walked over. "I have to say, Tippi, you do keep things interesting."

"I do my best," I said. Where was Hawk, though? This was it. Maybe this was his plan to get rid of me. It was going to be just like before. I'd start trusting him, think I'd been all wrong about him, and then he'd pull the rug out from under me.

"You looking for Hawk? He'll show," Oscar said. "Now stop scanning the horizon. You don't want the hags to see you getting crazy when they arrive. Need to portray confidence."

Easier said than done, but I straightened my shoulders and tried to put a good face on it.

Oscar squinted, staring at my head. "When did that start?"

"Not sure," I said, tucking some hair behind my ear. The streaks had grown substantially since the dome. There would be no missing them now.

As I continued to scan the perimeter, my eyes kept getting drawn back to Zark. There wasn't going to be a good time for this conversation, so I was better off getting it done.

"Give me a second. I've got to go talk to Zark." I walked away from Zab and Oscar.

Zark parted with his company, as if he had a sense I needed a private moment with him.

I tucked my hands in my pockets as I stood in front of him. "Thanks for coming after everything that's happened."

"I said I would," he responded in a gruffer-than-normal tone.

"I'm sorry about your boy. I'm guessing you already know what happened?" I asked. Word spread fast in Xest, and I'd slept an entire day away.

He nodded. I'd never seen Zark too choked up for words, but he was struggling to talk. "Hawk came by and explained what went down."

"I was there at the end," I said, hoping this part wouldn't be a surprise. When he didn't say anything, I continued, "Gregor wanted you to know he was sorry for hurting you. I wanted you to know he tried to save me in the end. He turned on them at the last moment. That's how he ended up trapped in the dome with me."

Zark's chin lifted. "He did?" Zark dragged in a shuddering breath.

"He died a hero." It was a fat lie, but at least he'd be able to hold his head up with his buddies. It was all I could give him.

With a whoosh of air, the hags' building appeared and all conversations fell silent.

"I've got to go," I said.

"Thank you."

I gave Zark a wave, hurrying over to where Lead Hag was already stepping outside of the building. Zab was waving me over, telling me to hurry up.

She looked about the area, silently counting heads before she looked at me like a professor about to tell you that you'd failed the most important exam of your life.

I stopped in front of her.

Her eyes ran the length of me, and then she paused to stare at my hair for a second. "Tippi, also known as the Whimsy witch who wasn't, also known as the Nowhere witch, please step inside."

Zab stepped forward. "She's allowed to have an audience to witness the trials."

Lead Hag looked over her shoulder, appearing even meaner than normal. "The door will remain open, but do not cross the threshold."

Just knowing I had Zab, Bibbi, Oscar, and Musso right there within eyesight helped. I walked in, and every head that could fit in the door did, along with more at the windows.

Lead Hag stopped in the middle of her room, beside her two sisters.

"Are you still employed?" Lead Hag asked.

"Yes. Actually, I have an even better job. I'm now a broker."

There was a lot of humming as they looked at each other. No one seemed overly impressed, but maybe a tad surprised?

Ringlets tapped the air. "And your residence? It's been brought to our attention you are no longer living at your previous address. That you were asked to leave."

"I'm also living at the broker's office, as I have in the past. It's quite convenient for work purposes."

The three hags looked at each other before Lead Hag stepped forward. "The first test is a time-reverse potion. Write whatever you need down on the parchment and it will be supplied. Anything you ask for has to be used. You have fifteen minutes to prepare it."

I glanced at the door, seeing Zab fighting with Oscar and Musso for space. I gave him a smile. He gave me a nod. I didn't know how he'd guessed, but he'd saved my ass.

I wrote the list of ingredients needed, each one appearing on the table as soon as it hit the parchment.

I added things to the cauldron, swinging the pot out enough that the fire partially grazed the edge but didn't scorch it, and stirred continuously. In a weird way, it was like making sauce, because you didn't want to burn it, except this one wouldn't taste good. At least, it smelled like it wouldn't.

When it started to simmer but not quite boil, I swung it off the fire and ladled it into a glass jar, and then corked it, holding it out to the hags.

"I'll try it," Lead Hag said.

"No, I'll try it," Ringlet said.

"I'm the oldest, I should try it," Tall Hag said, reaching to take the bottle from my hand.

Lead Hag grabbed it first. "Fine. We'll share."

"That's not going to do much," Ringlet whined.

"Well, it's that or nothing, because I'm not handing it over," Lead Hag said, uncorking the bottle.

"Fine." Tall Hag crossed her arms.

Ringlet said nothing but looked irritated.

Lead Hag took a sip. Before the bottle left her lips, Tall Hag was complaining. "You took more than your share."

"I did not. It's thick and gets stuck to the sides," Lead Hag said.

Tall Hag took the bottle and sipped, before handing it to Ringlet.

I'd made this before. I knew it worked because I'd bartered with Bautere, and he'd never complained. That didn't make it any easier to breathe at the moment. It took a few moments before the hags' skin seemed to tighten, and then a flush of blood pinked them up and gave their cheeks a rosier tinge. They turned to each other, nodding. They didn't look like spring chickens, but they'd split the bottle, and there was only so much a partial would do. Point was, it had worked. Instead of looking like they'd crawled out of a grave, they looked like they were nearing retirement age. It didn't soften their looks any, though. They were still one scary trio.

One hurdle down and an unknown amount to go. I could feel a bead of sweat dripping between my shoulder blades as I waited for what would come next. Would there be another test, or would they count my references? One glance at the door told me that Hawk still hadn't arrived. If he had, the crowd would've parted for him to let him have the best spot in the doorway.

And then there was no doorway. Me and the hags were outside.

"We'll need to see you in combat next," Lead Hag said.

I'd expected this. Nothing surprising.

Ringlets leaned closer. "This will be a fight to the death. Do you agree? If not, it will mean automatic deportation."

The crowd went silent.

Bautere had moved around the side and, with a nod, told me everything I needed. I was ready for this. I'd known it, but having him give the nod didn't hurt any. Whether I felt like it or not, I was ready. I'd practiced hard.

Still, to the death? Did I want to live here so much I'd bet my life on it? Then again, what kind of life had I had in Salem? I could do this.

"I agree."

There was a murmur behind me from my crowd.

"Any interference will be an immediate forfeiture," Lead Hag said loud enough that the farthest person could hear.

I'd worn leather pants that would offer some protection for scrapes and scratches and were soft enough to move in. I shed my jacket and tossed it to Zab. I'd rather bear the cold than die from being encumbered by the bulk.

Now it was time to see what I'd be fighting. The crowd was looking around as well.

Tall Hag raised her hand, and a small bat appeared on her palm. A tiny bat wasn't much of a fight, which meant only one thing.

The hag petted the small creature, cooing to it and looking at me. The thing squeaked and then lifted into the air. The squeak turned into an ear-piercing squeal as it grew a hundred times its size, maybe a few hundred. It was hard to measure, as I was diving behind a boulder while it swooped toward me, two claws aimed at my heart and fangs showing.

The boulder only gained me a few seconds, as the bat turned around and was already making its second pass.

Remain calm. If I panic, I die.

I was a protectorate, and even if I wasn't so hot at protecting myself, I had enough magic to beat this thing. The key was using my magic to disable it. Turn the situation. If I didn't want to kill this thing, what was the best thing to do for it, to protect it? Shrink it back into its smaller form and then plead that it wasn't kind to kill something so much weaker? It was either that or I'd be the dead one.

I had to nullify the magic the hag had used on it. I'd have to let the bat get close enough so that I could touch it and pull the magic from it.

It swooped again with its claws out, aimed straight for my heart. The crowd screamed as I dodged at the last moment, hoping I'd get an opportunity to grab it after the claws were past me.

Grabbing it was a risk as well. How long could I hold it before it killed me? I'd need at least a few moments. I had to get on its back somehow. If I could get to a higher perch, dodge its attack, I might be able to jump onto it.

The tree was my only hope. It wouldn't be able to come down at me from above because the canopy was too thick. If it flew underneath me...

I ran for the nearest tree as the thing squealed and dived. I made it halfway before I had to dive to the ground, rolling away. Its claws sank into the ground I'd just occupied.

I got to my feet again, while it was pulling its claws out. It must have appeared to the crowd as if I weren't fighting at all. I wouldn't turn their way; their looks of doubt and disappointment would only throw me off my game. I needed to keep going with my plan and stay focused.

I scrambled up into the tree, into the branches, where

it couldn't get a clear shot at me. And then I waited as it shrieked and poked. I leaned left and right, dodging its claws most of the time and taking a few scrapes at other times, all while feeling its hot breath on me as it roared. It would get frustrated soon, and then it would stop poking at me and fly beneath me.

I waited. It shrieked. I swayed, large branches blocking it. Still, I could feel the warmth of my blood on my legs, making my pants stick to them.

I stayed patient. It finally turned to try another angle, and when it did, it spread its wings right below me.

It was now or never. It was time to fight, to do my best. I wouldn't think of failure. I took a leap of faith. I was airborne for less than a second before slamming into its back. It dipped and squealed loud enough to burst eardrums.

It rotated, trying to throw off the nuisance it had found attached to it. I grabbed a wing in each hand, managing to hold on through a series of turns, inching up its body whenever I could gain some purchase. I continued methodically, until I wrapped my arms around its neck. Now the real work started. I was either going to be able to pull the magic from it or I'd have to choke it to death.

I glanced at the ground, waiting for a descent. If I did it too soon, we'd both end up dead. It headed downward, right toward the tree it was going to try to use it to scrape me off its back.

I closed my eyes, pulling at the magic I felt surging through it, pulling it into me.

It shrank in my grasp, and we were no longer flying but crashing to the ground, a small bat in my hands squeaking. I rolled as I hit, holding my hands out so I didn't crush the poor animal that was nothing but a weapon.

Battered and bruised, bleeding from cuts on my legs and arms, I stood with the small bat still wrapped in my hands.

The crowd roared as the hags stood speechless. It was clear now that they'd expected me to fail from the beginning. Maybe *wanted* me to fail. I wouldn't be surprised if they had struck a deal with the people who'd called them in the first place and turned me in. What had ruining my life paid?

I grabbed the bat's tiny head, making it look like I was going to break its neck.

"To the death, right?" I asked, as if needing clarification.

Two hags were stone-faced, but not Tall Hag.

"Perhaps we should handle that part," she said, walking forward, trying to take the bat from my hands.

"Are you sure?" I asked, hesitating to hand it over.

"Yes." She took her pet back, and the small bat crawled onto her shoulder and nestled in her hair.

Lead Hag looked at Ringlets and rolled her eyes before turning her attention back to me.

We were suddenly back in the cottage, and I could hear everyone scrambling to get a good spot in the door or a window.

"If you're an upstanding witch, why don't you have fifty character witnesses outside? That is a very strict requirement," Lead Hag asked.

"I do have fifty. One was late, but he's probably outside now." Hawk better be there. If he'd screwed me again, I'd find a way back from Salem, if only to kill him.

"I'm here," Hawk said, from the door at my back.

I closed my eyes for a second, trying to keep myself together. He'd shown. He hadn't hung me out to dry.

"We'll need to count them again," Ringlet said.

"Might take a while," Hawk said.

"And why is that Mr. Hawk?" Lead Hag asked.

"Quite a few more have shown."

"How many are there?" Tall Hag asked, as if outraged.

"Might be easier to come see for yourself," Hawk said. The hags ran out the door.

"Ye of little faith," Hawk whispered as I came close.

"Past tends to be future," I shot back, right before I walked outside. It was the last thing I was capable of saying, because in front of me was a crowd so big, it had to be half of Xest. Probably exactly half. It was every patron I'd ever waited on. Every client I'd made a deal with. It was every person who'd ever nodded at me as I passed them on the street. Even the witch who had the ghost who'd gotten me picked up on a bounty was here. They'd all come to be character witnesses.

"I told you he was coming," Oscar said as he walked over to me. "Hey, I thought you didn't cry?"

"I'm not crying." My eyes might've been watering, but if none of the tears escaped, it didn't happen.

"Getting a little too close for my tastes," he said, making a show of taking a large step away from me, smiling as he did.

The hags were looking about the place, talking to themselves and looking like they wanted to strangle someone.

Lead Hag turned to me. "We'll count the witnesses, but this doesn't mean you will be allowed to stay, considering the other situations we've been hearing about."

"We know what happened in the Unsettled Lands," Ringlet said.

I was getting tossed out. It was a setup. They were kicking me to the curb, back to Rest. They'd never intended to let me stay.

Hawk stepped forward. "There's a lot of people who are interested in hearing the outcome of this particular case from their *elected* immigration officials. When was the next election, by the way? Because I looked it up, and from what I saw, we're about a thousand years overdue."

The hags turned to each other, and even though I couldn't hear them, there was a lot of pointing, and it looked like they were yelling at each other.

Hawk walked up to them.

"I'd like a minute alone with you."

They stopped arguing and looked at him, then each other, as if debating if it was a good idea. Finally, Lead Hag gave a nod, and the three hags walked into the cottage with him.

Oscar walked over. "Don't worry. He's got ways to fix things. He'll handle it."

Zab stepped over to my other side. "He does."

The hags and Hawk walked back out of the cottage.

The Lead Hag stepped in front. "Tippi, the Whimsy witch who wasn't, also known as the Nowhere witch, is now an official resident of Xest, until the time of an unfortunate death or death by depletion of magic. Our ruling is final."

As soon as the words left her mouth, her and the cottage were gone.

A roar went through the crowd, as if they were as happy as I was. I looked around at the smiling and laughing faces and realized they were feeling some of the things bubbling inside me. And not just Zab and Musso, but all of them. Every time I'd gone up to someone and asked if they'd be a reference, something in me had knotted up; I'd feel like I was weighing them down with my issues.

Scanning the crowd now, that wasn't the case. They'd wanted to be here for me.

34

I walked downstairs, heading to the back room to get a tea, even though the Sweet Shop was still probably open at this time.

The monkeys broke into the *Rocky* theme as I passed. I gave them a slight nod and then tossed a loose coin from my pocket into their jar.

As I sipped my tea, Zab walked in and dropped down onto the other side of the couch.

"How are you doing?" he asked, smiling. "Been a busy couple of days."

"You know, I'm doing surprisingly well. Maybe you get used to being almost killed?" I sipped my tea and nibbled on one of the cookies I'd found in the station.

"Couldn't say." Zab stuck his bottom lip out slightly. "People don't typically try to kill me, but please, explain. I'd like to hear this." He turned slightly, sinking deeper into the couch and giving me his full attention.

"Well, it's strange. That first time, when the grouslies nearly killed me, I could barely think past the shock of it all. I might've tried to act okay, but I was rattled pretty bad."

He nodded. "I remember. You looked it."

"Then the dragon incident happened. That was pretty frightening. Then *it* had tried to get me to kill myself. Then Raydam, and the giant bat today. I'm starting to get the hang of this almost-getting-killed thing."

"You're doing very well at it, that's for certain."

"Yeah, I guess it just gets easier. Sure feels like it. I'm a little sore and tired, but there's none of that leftover shock. It's more along the lines of: yeah, they want me dead. Now I want them dead, and let's just get on with things."

Zab tilted his head back and laughed. "You know, you sound a little like Hawk right now."

Knowing Hawk, they'd probably tried to kill him way more times than me. It made sense.

Musso walked in, followed by Bibbi.

"You did good today, kid," he said with a look that was bursting with pride, like I was his daughter.

"Thanks, Musso."

"Amazing," Bibbi said, taking the seat beside me. "And your hair is totally rocking."

"Thanks, Bibbi." How had I ever disliked this girl?

"There's the superstar," Oscar said, walking in. "You killed it today."

"Thanks, Oscar."

We spent the next couple of hours rehashing every moment of the day until, one by one, they got up and went home. I didn't have to go anywhere. I already was home.

But I had another errand that had to be done before I could go to sleep.

I got up to grab my jacket from the front office but paused. Using just enough magic to not set anything else on fire, I lit a candle. I put it on my desk and sat down, looking about the place. Things were going to get rough around here, worse than they'd ever been. I'd felt true evil, and it was coming for me. I couldn't say I regretted coming back, though, not even for a second. This was where I was supposed to be. I'd spent enough years trying to swim upstream to know when I'd found my place.

A slip shot out of Helen, tumbled in the air, and landed on my desk, face-up.

Hawk wasn't the back cloud. It was me.

"I should've known." I pocketed the note as I laughed. I wasn't mad, not even a little. That black cloud had helped me get back here. "It's okay. It worked out for the best."

Another slip shot out.

I might've had something to do with Braid and Spike abducting you as well.

"Thank you." I pocketed that one to save as well. When the all-knowing wish machine thought you should be here, it had to be so. "Anything else you want to confess?"

I waited, but there were no more slips or gears.

"I'll be back. Going to go take a walk around as a formal citizen before I call it a night. See what might be lurking before I hit the hay."

Helen's gears ground before she went silent.

"Night to you too."

I threw on my jacket, stepping out into the cold, the fifth wind tearing through the fabric like I was dressed in silk, my boots hitting the pavement with the confident thud of someone who didn't care who heard them.

The streets were quieter than normal but sizzled with tension, as the people who were out eyed each other as if they were going to be possible combatants in the octagon. Whatever crude civilization Xest had was going to take a real beating, as the feeling of *it* filled these streets. The divide had already been here when I first arrived, a lost soul who didn't know who she was, or what she was. Everything was changing. The person I'd been was a shadow of the woman I was becoming. This place, so strange and yet so rigid in its beliefs, was changing too. Into what? I didn't know.

Where before, people from the other side of the line politely ignored each other, now you feared a knife in your back if you made the error of losing sight of them. I was getting bolder and harder myself, and it was just in the nick of time.

The line in the snow, the one everyone would have to choose a side, was now a chasm separating us. A war was coming, and I knew what side I was on. I knew I was going to have to shed any softness that might still be clinging to me. If I was going to survive, if Xest was going to survive, I'd have to become as savage as that thing I'd managed to corral for a time.

Familiar footsteps sounded behind me, but I didn't need to look over my shoulder to see who it was. Hawk fell into step right beside me.

Hawk and I had our differences, but he had my back—when it counted and our goals aligned, anyway. Right now? They couldn't have been any more in sync.

"Nice night for a quick patrol," he said.

"I thought so."

As we walked, I could feel a trace of its power all around. It hadn't been idle in captivity. It had grown—a lot. This was what my freedom had cost.

"You know, it would've been smarter to let me die in that dome." I wasn't sure why I was saying it other than it was the truth. I didn't like it, but Xest might've been better off if I'd died in that dome. Except Hawk would've died there with me, and I didn't seem capable of *not* saving him.

"I've made many worse decisions than that." He smiled.

I looked at him, wondering if he might've been admitting to a little regret about forcing me out.

He continued, "It's going to get ugly here. No one would fault you for leaving if you have any doubts."

I was laughing now. "You must be kidding. After what I went through to stay? No. This is my home."

"I know it is. You belong here."

Something inside me stilled at hearing him utter those words. Sometimes you don't know what you're waiting to hear, or need to hear, until you hear it. But him saying that seemed to cement my place as firmly as the hags had. I was no longer the Nowhere witch. I was Tippi, from Xest —the most feared man here had declared it, so how could it be anything but true?

"Are you going to tell me what you said to the hags that changed their minds? I do appreciate the help. I'm just curious how you managed to pull it off," I said.

"Let's just say that the timing isn't quite right to discuss, but it had to be done if you were going to stay."

"Feel like sharing with me what the hell you changed into the other day?"

"Again, the timing might not be quite right," he said, smiling.

"Give me one answer, then. How did you know I was going to have a problem with immigration?"

"Considering that half of Xest doesn't care for you, it wasn't much of a leap. I knew about it since the morning the note was on your door, and I had some time to line a few things up."

"Is that why..." No, there was no way he'd forced me back to the broker's building just for my sake. I'd already given him way too much credit. I wasn't giving him any more. Bad things happened when I put Hawk on a pedestal that high.

"What?" he asked.

"Forget it. The timing isn't quite right," I said.

He laughed at my use of his answer.

"Just so you know, I don't thank people when I'm not sure what they did." Whatever he had done, I was surely going to pay a price for it at some point in the future.

"You're welcome," he said, as if I'd thanked him anyway.

He wasn't going to tell me what he did, and I wasn't going to pursue it, because right now, I had too much on my plate, and the battle lines had been drawn with him on my side. Yeah, I trusted him, at least in keeping me here, and maybe keeping me alive. If a fight came down, he'd be the first to have my back. That he'd proven, and that was enough. In times like these, it might mean every-thing, because there were some dark times ahead.

The heaviness was palpable, a sizzle in the air as you waited for that first strike of lightning to commence the storm. I knew darkness. I'd grown up with darkness, and things were about to get pitch-black.

There was only one thing I didn't know for sure, and it was the only question that mattered right now, the one that would keep me up tonight, and every night after: in the fight for Xest's future, who would be the victor? Would the good guys win like they did in the fairytales of Rest? Or would this tale have a darker ending? As this was officially my home now, I was going to find out.

Read The Most Wanted Witch, the next installment of Tales of Xest, now.

Text Augustine to 22828 to get Donna Augustine new release notifications.

Or, follow me on one of these platforms:
http://www.donnaaugustine.com
Twitter handle: @DonnAugustine
https://www.facebook.com/groups/223180598486878/

ACKNOWLEDGMENTS

No book would be complete without a thanks to the crew who helps me get each story over that final hurdle. Donna Z., Lisa A, Camilla J., Lori H., Tammy K., Christine J. and Ashleigh M., every one of you has added something to this story. Thank you for sticking with me!

ALSO BY DONNA AUGUSTINE

Ollie Wit

A Step into the Dark

Walking in the Dark

Kissed by the Dark

The Keepers

The Keepers

Keepers and Killers

Shattered

Redemption

Karma

Karma

Jinxed

Fated

Dead Ink

The Wilds

The Wilds

The Hunt

The Dead

The Magic

Born Wild (Wilds Spinoff)

Wild One

Savage One

Wyrd Blood

Wyrd Blood

Full Blood

Blood Binds